The Sheikh's Hidden Heart

Sands of Passion, Volume 4

Amara Holt

Published by Amara Holt, 2024.

Copyright © 2024 by Amara Holt

All rights reserved.

No part of this book may be reproduced, distributed, or transmitted in any form or by any means, including photocopying, recording, or other electronic or mechanical methods, without the prior written permission of the author, except in the case of brief quotations in book reviews.

This is a work of fiction. Names, characters, places, and incidents are the product of the author's imagination or are used fictitiously. Any resemblance to actual events, organizations, locales, or persons, living or dead is coincidental and is not intended by the authors.

PROLOGUE

Ayda

ONE YEAR BEFORE...

I descend the last flight of stairs, listening to the muffled voices coming from the living room.

I lower my head, knowing that we have guests but unsure if there are any men present, so I put on my *hijab*.

"Come in, dear," I hear Aunt Zenda's cheerful voice.

I walk toward her, keeping my smile restrained on my lips, lowering my face slightly in a brief greeting.

"Hello, Aunt," I murmur.

"Sit down," she points to the empty couch next to my mother, "I have good news."

I sit beside my mother, keeping my fingers clasped in my lap.

"I hope they are good," my father huffs.

I know he hates it when Aunt Zenda comes to brag about her luxurious life, as if she takes pleasure in rubbing it in our faces.

"Well, brother, you ungrateful fool, I said I would help marry off my nieces, and it's time to put them on the market, so to speak. The emir wants to marry, or rather, we'll make sure he does. Ayda will spend a few days with me at the Zabeel palace, and I'll make sure Hassan proposes to her."

I can hear a dreamy sigh from my mother's side.

An emir?

I almost let out a laugh, but every time I think about acting recklessly, I remember all the times my father punished me, making it clear that I am a lady and must behave as such.

I say nothing; no one asked for my opinion—they've already mapped out my future.

I can even hear Aunt Zenda organizing my marriage to the ruler of Budai.

I never aspired to a grand marriage, nor did I want anything luxurious. I just want to leave this house. But when I think about the possibility of finding a worse husband than my father once I leave, a shiver runs down my spine.

I just wanted to date and get to know my future husband better, but I know that won't be the case.

I'm already 23 and still single; all my flirtations didn't work out because Aunt Zenda intervened in all of them, saying that my sisters and I deserved a blue-blooded Sheikh. Of course, Mom and Dad believed her, being swayed by her words.

As for me? Does it matter when all I've been taught is to obey my future husband?

All my school friends are already married, and many of them tried to introduce me to their relatives, but for Ayda, no one is good enough, or at least, that's how my aunt makes it seem.

Zenda is my father's sister and, miraculously, caught the attention of the emir and became his second wife. Now that her husband has passed away, she wants to push me onto his son, the current emir of Budai.

"Ayda, dear, shall we go?" my aunt asks without giving me a choice.

I nod in response, receiving a look of approval from my father.

Esmail, my father, raised me to serve my husband. His voice is etched in my mind:

Ayda, manners.
Ayda, don't speak loudly.

Ayda, lower your head.
Ayda, married women don't look at other men.
Ayda, follow your mother's example...

Always the same instructions: how to behave impeccably. The typical woman who simply obeys.

Every time I look at my mother, I get a fleeting daydream of what my future will be like. Will it be the same as hers?

Sometimes I wish I had been born a man so that I could look around without fear, without someone reprimanding me.

I don't even come from a wealthy family, but I know my parents want the same thing that happened with Aunt Zenda—a luxurious marriage.

I come from a family of handkerchief traders, nothing to be proud of, as we're the lowest of Budai, even though we have a good financial standing.

Of course, with Aunt Zenda living in the Zabeel palace, we have good visibility, though it's not something to be proud of, as the Bughdadi are of the people, they don't help anyone due to blood ties, and they are always honest.

I bid farewell to my parents knowing I'll have to subject myself once again to the absurdity of going to that palace.

I have a great respect for the royal family of Budai, but I'm mortified at the thought of going there repeatedly, especially since they all know my aunt's intentions.

But what can I do? This is my fate: to find a good husband, even if I don't want to.

CHAPTER ONE

Ayda

PRESENT DAYS...

"Foolish girl," Aunt Zenda pulls me by the arm, dragging me out of the room.

I grimace at the pain. I enter the room with my cousin Elahe by my side.

"Ungrateful family, after everything I've done for them, this is what I get, being expelled from my own home?" Aunt Zenda releases my arm.

I look at my cousin, who has a look of pity.

"Mom, I think it's better if you leave before Hassan gets angry," Elahe murmurs.

"He is the most ungrateful. The deal was for you to marry him," Zenda looks at me.

"Aunt, my marriage to Abdul is the most suitable for the moment," I murmur.

"No! He is not the emir, he is the emir's brother. We wanted the best, not his shadow."

"Mom, Abdul might be the best choice. We wouldn't want her to marry a man who would hate her every day," Elahe argues.

"Does it matter? He just needs to know that Ayda is better than that little thing Malika," Aunt Zenda twists her lip.

When Abdul proposed, I almost thanked Allah. From the beginning, he was the one who caught my attention, even though he never cast a glance at me.

Hassan is always so serious; it's clear from his eyes that he is in love with Malika, the wife meant to be his. I would just be a thorn in their side.

Abdul is the elder brother of the emir of Budai; they are half-brothers to my cousin Elahe, from their father's first marriage.

"Aunt, you succeeded; you got me inside the palace, here I am," I murmur, holding onto the edge of my *hijab*.

"But that wasn't the goal..." Zenda sighs in frustration.

"Cousin, are you happy?" Elahe asks.

"Yes," I whisper, looking at the two of them.

"How can you be happy with this? After all, we are talking about Abdul."

"Abdul is a discreet man and has no intentions of taking a second wife. He is not intrusive and has all the qualities of being a great friend to Ayda. What could be better than that? Mom, we're talking about Abdul, an upstanding man. He may be a mystery, given that he's 37 and has never thought of marrying, but he is the right choice. Hassan would never be the ideal man for Ayda; he drags a truck for Malika, capable of buying the world to see his wife smile—they are in love."

Elahe speaks the truth. Anyone in their right mind can see it; the emir of Budai is crazy about his wife. In a way, I envy that; I wish for something like that for myself, a true love, something that doesn't need words. Just by their looks, it's clear they love each other.

I would never be the ideal second wife for Hassan. I didn't want this, but my opinion has never mattered to anyone.

"Come on, Ayda, let's leave this palace," Aunt Zenda calls me.

"Let me take my cousin home," Elahe offers.

"Are you going to stay in this palace?" My aunt refers to her daughter.

"I believe so," Elahe shrugs her shoulders slightly.

"Good, then I'll have someone to be my eyes and ears here," Zenda says confidently, turning her back. "Don't think I've forgotten what you did, Ayda."

Aunt Zenda spoke without turning to face us. After all, she will never accept that I said yes to Abdul.

"Sometimes I wish I had the confidence she has," Elahe murmurs.

"She has quite a temperament," I murmur.

"I think she has several temperaments," my cousin jokes.

I turn my face towards her.

"No one in this palace likes me; I don't know how I'll live here without Aunt Zenda, and soon, you'll be married off too," I bite my lip nervously.

"I believe you and Malika could be good friends. When you move to Zabeel, you won't have my mother interfering in your life. The biggest obstacle has always been my mother."

I nod; Elahe stops beside me, and I link my arm with hers.

We walk together down the palace corridor.

"Does it hurt?" Elahe points to my arm.

"Aunt has quite a heavy hand," I murmur, feeling the slight burn in my arm.

"Tell me about it; she did that to me several times," my cousin glances over her *hijab*.

"Aren't you nervous about your marriage, cousin?" I ask.

"Very much so, especially with him being another Sheikh. I wish he were just an ordinary man, without titles, without the same burden I have." She lets out a long sigh.

We enter the room where everyone is still present, except the emir and his wife. The whispers stop as we enter the room.

"Has my mother left?" Elahe asks.

"Yes, she and the girls," Maya, the first wife of the deceased emir, answers.

Maya is the first wife, Aunt Zenda is the second, and the third wife does not live in the palace. In total, the emir had 22 children from the three wives.

My eyes wander around the room, meeting Abdul's gaze. Even though he has never shown interest in marrying, he has always been the brother who caught my attention, even though to him I must seem uninteresting. I have always heard many whispers that I am uninteresting, without personality, and that I was born to be a shadow, a typical decoration. What no one knows is that I was trained to be this way.

Unlike the other brother, he has a more relaxed demeanor but always with the same evaluative look, as if he were observing everything.

His intense, dark eyes angled to the side, thick dark hair, and a dense beard marking his face: the epitome of an Arab man.

My gaze follows his hand as it rises to his beard, scratching it. The action makes me realize that I was staring at him too much. I lower my face as a sign of intimacy, and thus, would be violating the rules imposed upon me.

"I'll take Ayda home..." Elahe breaks my reverie.

"Alright, dear," Maya responds again.

"Your father has been informed about our engagement; he will come to the palace tomorrow," Abdul's masculine voice is present.

I raise my face to look at the man, not knowing whether I should respond to him or how I should behave in front of him.

My parents have deprived me of so many things that now I feel like a fool.

"Alright, brother," Elahe responds.

I see Abdul roll his eyes and leave the room with a long sigh.

My cousin guides me out of the room.

"I'm so pathetic," I murmur as soon as we are alone.

"It will be fine; I'll ask Abdul to be patient with you," she says with comforting words.

"May *Allah* hear you, cousin, because I don't know how to react in the presence of my husband," I whisper with fear.

CHAPTER TWO

Ayda

ONE MONTH LATER...

"Daughter" I turn my face, my white dress swaying as I move. My mother walks towards me. "We need to talk" I notice she's unsure how to start the conversation.

Mom intertwines her hand with mine as we walk towards a door.

After the four days of wedding festivities, I find myself exhausted; I never imagined it could be so tiring.

Abdul barely looks my way, and the few times he does, he gives me a look of pity, as if he feels sorry for me.

Raja opens a private door for me to enter, and I go in before her.

"Daughter, I'm calling you for this talk because I need you to know that your father and I are very happy with this union, but you also need to remember that you have a family and that before taking any action, you should consider how it might affect us. Be faithful to your husband and completely submissive to his desires."

I blink several times. Do I really need to hear this even on the day of my wedding?

"Okay, Mom..." I murmur.

"Ayda, always keep your voice low, never speak louder than him, respect him, and remember that he comes from a much higher position than ours."

Yes, Mom, I know, I must be the perfect wife.

"Yes, Mom" I nod again, agreeing with everything she has said.

"I think that's it; I believe you know everything you need to about your wedding night already..." Her face turns a shade of red.

"Yes, I know" I murmur, recalling the instructions she gave me.

Raja made it clear that I shouldn't look it up online, but curiosity got the better of me given the words she used, and, well, it was quite instructive and a bit strange.

If it's like that, maybe I won't know how to act. *Who am I kidding? If it's any way, I won't know how to act!*

My mother indicates that we should leave the room. I follow her, my dress trailing on the floor.

The weight of the ring on my finger makes it clear that I am now a married woman with the dream of every Arab woman: a good and exemplary family man.

We exit the room, and there are many dancers, women smiling amidst their conversations.

I approach my twin sisters, who are next to my cousins, and Aunt Zenda is with them. Of course, she's not happy with this union, even though Abdul is a wealthy Sheikh, it's not enough for her.

"I still think it's a waste; look at her beauty, she should be given to the richest man in this emirate" Aunt Zenda grabs my chin.

"Sister-in-law, we are all happy with the union you've arranged for our girl" Mom says with a smile on her lips.

"You settle for so little" Zenda scoffs.

I shift my weight onto one foot, feeling the throbbing pain in my legs.

I look around for my cousin Elahe, but I spot my husband's eyes instead. He, wearing a white suit, has dark hair contrasting with his skin and a neatly trimmed beard.

Abdul walks towards me, his steps determined, gently maneuvering around the guests.

I swallow hard when he stops beside me.

"Excuse me" he asks with an authoritative voice.

"What do you intend to do?" My aunt asks, crossing her arms.

"I'm going to take my wife for a walk" he says casually.

"The party isn't over yet; you can't take her away from here..."

"Not only can I, but I will" he nods his head.

I quickly glance at my mother, she nods. As I turn my body, I hear my aunt grumbling.

Abdul walks ahead of me, exiting through the back of the party, finding a corridor where several people are watching us, puzzled.

"Keep following me" he looks over his shoulder.

I nod, quickening my pace to keep up with him.

Abdul turns down one corridor and then another. He clearly knows this palace well, moving with precision, and slows his steps as he enters an empty corridor.

"We're married..." he lets the sentence trail off, putting his hand in his pocket and turning towards me after he stops walking.

I nod silently and look around.

"You can relax, no one comes this way; we're alone." He seems to have read my mind.

Abdul looks at me for long seconds as if trying to figure out what's going on with me.

"Do you want this marriage, Ayda?" he raises an eyebrow slightly "Everything will be easier if you speak..."

Abdul seems to be losing a bit of patience with my few words.

"Yes..." I murmur.

"Really?" He seems to doubt.

"Yes, I do."

"Great, we've established that. This will be our first night together; you know what I'm talking about?"

"Yes, I know..."

Abdul takes two steps towards me, stopping right in front of me, and takes his hand out of his pocket.

"I was going to ask if you're pure, but it's clear from your look that you are" he holds my chin, gently lifting my face.

I don't say anything, my eyes wide, waiting for his movements.

"I didn't want this marriage" he murmurs.

"I don't judge you" I whisper as his face lowers towards mine.

"We need to discuss a few things about our marriage; I don't want a copy of Zenda by my side" his breath collides with my face.

His lip touches mine so softly, brushing against them.

"And there's more" he murmurs.

I instinctively close my eyes as he speaks, touching my lip with his and moistening my lips.

"What's wrong?" I ask, not sure where my voice came from.

Abdul raises his hand, brushing his fingers on my cheek. I open my lips, missing his against them.

"We'll only have this night together, a mere act to take your virginity. It will stain the sheets, and after tonight, there will be nothing more between us; we'll just share the same room for a few days..." he speaks so decisively, shattering the magic of the moment.

"But, but..." I don't understand.

"I don't want this marriage; I have another woman, and since she can't be acknowledged, know that we will only be a façade of a couple."

At that moment, my world collapses as if a hole had opened in my legs and I was falling into freefall.

CHAPTER THREE

Ayda

I said goodbye to my family, knowing that the next step is to be alone with my husband. His words constantly echo in my mind. A marriage entirely for show, he has a mistress, and I will be the official wife while he maintains an extramarital relationship with another woman. What I don't understand is what's stopping him from marrying that woman instead.

Abdul walked beside me, remaining silent. I hold up my dress to climb the stairs, walking behind my husband.

He is tall, and even though I am tall too, I don't reach his height.

Stopping in front of a door, he opens it, pushing it to the side and giving me the opportunity to enter first.

"In this first week, we will spend every night together," he whispers, closing the door behind him "after that, we'll see if you'll go to your own room."

I didn't say anything, what can I say, demand that he be only mine? This is different from having a husband with more than one wife, as, before our *Allah,* he has obligations to all his wives. Abdul is betraying me and makes a point of rubbing it in my face.

I am outraged and was not instructed to endure this.

"If I make a cut, we could say the act is consummated" I say while walking around the room.

The dim light in the room could make everything more romantic, if not for a small obstacle.

"Are you serious?" Abdul lets out a low, sarcastic laugh.

"If I am so loathsome in your eyes, we don't need to perform the act" I glance over my shoulder.

Abdul is standing by the bed with his hand in his pants pocket.

"I wish I could say the same..."

"What's stopping you?" I turn my body, raising my arm and removing the pins that hold my headscarf in place.

I tilt my head to the side, trying to see where the pin had caught. I am startled when I feel Abdul's large hand over mine, removing the pin, and then the others. With ease, he takes off the *hijab* from my head, letting my long hair cascade down my shoulders, and I step away from my husband.

"You'll have to get pregnant at some point; that's the big obstacle. No sex, no children..." he whispers the words close to me.

"We could say I have problems" I shrug.

"This is madness, why all this refusal?"

I say nothing, only avert my gaze from his, continuing to walk, wanting to keep my distance, but his hand pulls me by my wrist, making me stumble over my own foot and cling to his chest. I lift my face, my hair falling over it.

"I don't see the need to consummate something that doesn't suit either of us" I whisper, trying to straighten my body, but he holds tightly to my waist.

As if I weighed only a gram, he turns me around, and his fingers go straight to the buttons of my dress.

"We're going to consummate this marriage; I don't do things halfway" he declares, pushing my hair to the side.

Abdul unbuttons the last button of the dress, sliding the fabric down my shoulder. His touch causes a slight tingling wherever he goes, until the dress falls to the floor, leaving me only in the thin fabric of my nightgown underneath.

I lift one foot at a time, stepping out from the dress. I turn my body and see Abdul removing his jacket and then the white shirt from inside his pants.

His eyes meet mine with a slight narrowing, frowning at my curiosity.

He stops what he's doing and approaches me.

I shrink away as he stands in front of me, and holding my chin, he lifts my face.

"Why are you always so reserved?"

"I'm cautious" I murmur.

"There shouldn't be secrets between a couple..."

"There shouldn't be a third person who doesn't belong between a couple" I widen my eyes at the words that escaped without thinking.

He lets a smile slip across his lips.

"So that's it, when you're honest, it's better."

I roll my eyes, knowing it's easy for him to judge.

"Are you rolling your eyes, wife?" Abdul furrows his brow.

"Sorry" I whisper against my will.

"You wanted to apologize?"

"No!" I am honest.

"Great..."

His hand goes to my neck, gripping my hair at the nape, and he tightens his hold with such force that I let out a sigh of pain.

"I hate when people roll their eyes at me, I hate any bodily expression of defiance..."

Abdul lowers his lip, touching mine with delicacy, his beard brushing against my face. I let myself be carried away by the moment, mimicking his movements, opening my mouth, allowing his tongue to explore mine, wrapping around it. I can feel my legs growing weak.

"We can make this first time good, or..." he murmurs amid the kiss.

"Or what?"

"There is no second option; I would never take it against your will, but I can make you want it."

"I don't want to" I plead in a whisper.

"Are you sure?" he holds both sides of my face.

"I don't want to know that I have to share my husband with a mistress..."

"After all, you have your own opinions, and I thought you were a great fool" he always mocks and belittles the fact that there is another woman.

I huff during the kiss, an act that is enough for him to lift me into his lap.

His hand holds my back, soon tossing me onto the middle of his bed.

"Did you huff at me? Is that what I heard?" he declares seriously while unbuttoning his shirt.

"I'm not a child to be treated as one" I murmur, my eyes fixed on his deft fingers unfastening the buttons.

He lets out a weak laugh, tossing the shirt onto the floor and revealing his chest, with a few black hairs, a large abdomen marked by a flat stomach. I know he likes sports and is always practicing with his brother.

He unbuttons his pants and lets the fabric fall to his feet, revealing white underwear that I don't look at directly, turning my face to the side. I bite my lip.

I always idealized this moment, but it was never like this, knowing that I am an obligation for my husband.

"Get up" Abdul asks.

Bracing myself on my elbows, I rise, holding onto his hand.

I stand in front of him, his hands holding the hem of my nightgown, pulling it over my head.

I close my eyes before my naked body and his assessing gaze.

"Has no one ever seen you like this?" he asks with a husky voice.

"Except for my mother?" I open my eyes to find his gaze fixed on my breast.
"So I'm the first?" I nod "Has any man ever touched you?"
"No" I murmur.
"Not even kissed you?"
"No..."
"Was that your first kiss?" He asks, amazed.
"Yes..."
"Damn, it shouldn't be like this..." Abdul lets out a long sigh, closing his eyes and then reopening them.
"What? Saving myself for my husband?"
"Another man should have marked you, so it would become insignificant, but knowing I'll be the first might sound a bit controlling... Knowing that all of this belongs only to my eyes and that only my lips will be marked in your memory makes me a damned possessive."

Abdul pulls me by the waist, his tight grip marking my skin. He lowers his face to kiss my shoulder. Gently, he lays me on the bed, his lips trailing down, kissing every piece of skin, stopping at my breast. I close my eyes and feel his tongue there, circling my nipple. He moves down my belly, causing a pleasant tingling, and my skin is on fire.

Abdul positions himself over my leg when I open it, leaving me exposed to him.

"Fuck..." he whispers so softly it comes out as a breath "I need to feel this."

Before I had a chance to intervene, his mouth is on my pussy, licking it all over. *That... that...*

Words fail me, and having him there in that way makes everything so intimate.

"Abdul..." I murmur his name, raising my hand to touch his silky, soft hair.

"No, you're not going to come like this" he murmurs, standing up "look to the side."

He asks, and I comply while I hear him lowering the fabric of his underwear, then coming back on top of me.

"I didn't want you to see to avoid making you tense" he declares, his face in front of mine.

I feel his member brushing my entrance, the one that will break my virginity. I will be marked by him.

"This will hurt, but it's necessary" Abdul warns, bringing his lips to mine.

I feel him filling me in a slow motion, going all the way in. I feel discomfort, as if I'm being invaded.

I grip his shoulder tightly, digging my nails in.

"Shhh, soon the discomfort will pass" he whispers with a soft voice.

He lifts his face, his hand caressing my face, our eyes locked on each other. As he moves in and out, the rhythm becomes more frequent, a steady back and forth. The torture also starts to turn sweet.

When he notices that my breathing has eased, he lowers his face, taking me in a kiss, intensifying the movements.

His fingers take the middle of our bodies, stimulating my pussy, making me sigh amidst the kiss.

He doesn't stop, and the discomfort passes briefly.

I close my eyes and feel a wave pass through my body, surrendering to it, writhing underneath him.

"Ah... fuck..." I was filled with hot spurts.

Abdul gives one last thrust, collapsing on top of me.

Our chests have an uncontrolled rhythm as we wait for our breathing to return to normal.

Soon, he gets up, and I can feel the emptiness of his body.

His eyes went straight to the middle of my legs, as if confirming that I was indeed pure. *Asshole*!

He doesn't say anything, just turns his back and goes to the bathroom, leaving me there, alone. If I have ever felt such humiliation, nothing compares to this.

CHAPTER FOUR

Abdul

I leave the bathroom and find the bed empty. Where did this woman go? My feet drag on the floor, stopping beside the bed, where I see a red stain on the white sheet, confirming that she was indeed pure. I turn my body as I see the night breeze making the curtain move, noting that the door is open.

I furrow my brow and head over there. I see the silhouette of my wife on the balcony, her long hair cascading down her back, the gentle breeze causing some strands to move. A robe covers her body; outside, the night is dark, with no lights, and my room overlooks the empty side of the palace.

I watch the girl for a long time, hearing her let out a long sigh. Perhaps Ayda isn't so bad; maybe she has a bit of personality. But I promised Sadira I would keep this marriage purely a facade.

No one knows about my involvement with her, not even my brother. If Hassan knew, I don't know how he would react, knowing that Sadira was my father's third wife and the mother of his children. Now she is involved in a forbidden affair with me.

I don't know what I have with her, but it's something simple, where we both know it's just about pleasure. After my father's death, I was going back and forth between the Zabeel palace and the palace where she lives with my brothers.

On one of those occasions, amid our sadness, we found our pleasure. Since then, we have had sporadic meetings, just to satisfy our bodies, knowing that all of this is forbidden.

When Hassan declared that I would marry Ayda, I was furious to know that I would have a woman to whom I would have to be accountable, unable to disappear or be unseen.

Damn! I didn't want this marriage. It was a part of my freedom that went with it.

My feet drag to the balcony, catching her attention, and she turns her face, looking at me through her hair. Her black hair forms a curtain.

She doesn't say anything, always very silent.

One cannot deny, Ayda is beautiful. Her delicate face, the upturned nose, the eyes with a brown hue containing some yellowish spots.

Beautiful would be an understatement for her beauty.

I approach her body. She turns her silhouette, looking me in the eyes.

"How are you?" I ask.

"Does it really matter?" she doesn't answer, her voice carrying that low tone.

"If I'm asking, it must," I cross my arms in front of my bare chest.

She lowers her gaze, focusing on the waistband of my pants.

"I'm fine, thanks for your concern," I can sense a hint of sarcasm in her voice.

"Away from your aunt, I see you have a sharp tongue after all," I raise my eyebrow as I see her shiver from the cool breeze.

"I thought you didn't want someone like her... If you prefer, I can be quiet," Ayda looks towards the door to the room, perhaps considering the idea of entering.

"Do you want to come in?" I gesture with my head and she nods.

Without saying a word, she enters the room, and I'm left alone on the balcony. I can hear her closing the suite door. Soon the shower starts making noise; she's taking a bath.

I grip the edge of the balcony made of cement and look out at the night.

Of all the things I could imagine within this marriage, one of them was not written anywhere: the fact that I liked being inside her, desiring every part of her body, almost coming immediately when my cock entered her tight little pussy.

Fuck, it was so much easier not to desire her when she wasn't mine.

But now I desire her, as if she were a new flavor, because when we don't know the taste, it's easy to ignore, but once we discover how delicious it is, it's hard to ignore.

How to ignore the fact that I have a wife completely at my disposal, beautiful, sexy, full of curves, knowing that I can do whatever I want with her, and yet I have a mistress.

By *Allah*, what will I do? I know that our great *Allah* is not the most appropriate to call at this moment since what I'm doing is wrong.

Especially now, being married. Damn, damn, damn...

I want to fuck Ayda, I want her under me, I want her on top of me, I want this woman in every way, crying out my name.

But I've already started off on the wrong foot; I've already revealed to her that I have a mistress. Maybe this isn't the best way to start a marriage. But that was the truth.

Sadira asked me to continue my meetings with her. She asked that this marriage be purely a facade since I always complained about how Ayda was a perfect copy of her aunt.

That was until I was alone with her. *Until I liked hearing her voice. Hell*!

I let out a long sigh, hearing the bathroom door open. Perhaps I've spent too much time musing about my wife, whom I thought was completely dull.

I turn my body, seeing Ayda enter our closet. I go back into the room and follow her steps. I stop at the closet door, where I watch her distractedly, not noticing my presence.

She removes her robe, revealing her curves, medium-sized, slightly upturned breasts with beautiful, erect nipples that I wanted to bite just to hear her moan.

Ah, damn, my eyes land on her smooth little pussy.

I can feel my cock starting to weigh in my pants, instinctively growing hard at the thought of fucking her again.

Ayda walks around the room, letting her long hair, which had been pinned up, fall down her back, contrasting with her slightly tanned skin. *That skin tone is so perfect, it suits her so well.*

Her fingers graze the fabrics, picking up a blue nightgown.

"No clothes," I say, not recognizing the hoarse tone in my throat, forcing myself to moisten my mouth.

Ayda is startled, turning her body towards me, quickly trying to cover her nakedness.

"Too late, I've already seen you naked, wife, analyzed every piece of your skin, even your smooth pussy," I'm being a jerk just to see her face flush.

"I'm not going to sleep naked." Ayda's eyes widen.

"Oh, come on, I'm the one who makes the rules."

I walk towards her, grabbing her arm and easily placing her over my shoulder with her buttocks completely exposed to me. And I spank her hard.

"Ow!" Ayda complains as I lay her down on the bed.

"Every time we sleep together, I want you like this," I point to her body.

"Naked?" Her innocence reflects in her eyes.

"Yes!"

"I thought you didn't want anything to do with me," She pouts in her natural way, which makes me want to bite her.

"I don't want to; I just don't want clothes in this bed," Of course, I lied.

That was the best strategy I could think of, to have her naked before my eyes.

"So where will you sleep?"

"In the same bed as you," I frown, not understanding.

"But you're dressed, does this rule only apply to me?"

"Smart girl..."

Without hesitation, I lower the fabric of my pants. My cock is grateful for the freedom. My eyes focus on Ayda's reaction. She tried to be bold, but her face flushed so much that it turned completely red.

I run my hand along the length of my penis.

"Do you like what you're seeing?" I ask, seeing an *Oh!* form on her lips.

Ayda swallowed and blinked several times, pulling a sheet and covering her body. She didn't say anything. Maybe she was left speechless.

"I think it's better if we go to sleep," I finally say.

My cock can manage with just one time, as I refuse to give in to her untouched pussy by another man.

"Yeah..." My wife doesn't know what to say.

Sometimes it seems like she wants to say something but holds back, as if she has a block. I pull the blanket, lying down underneath it and sharing it with my wife.

Her floral scent fills my nostrils.

By *Allah*, I hope I don't get used to this scent.

Ayda needs to be just a facade wife!

CHAPTER FIVE

Ayda

My eyelids feel heavy, and I sense something pressing down on me, suffocating me. I quickly open my eyes and realize it's the strong hands of my husband causing this. Maybe I'm not used to sharing a bed with someone, especially someone being my husband, a man.

He holds me tightly, as if he doesn't want me to leave.

How can I make him loosen his grip? Waking up next to someone is so strange.

I move as if it's natural, closing my eyes again, pretending to be in some dream, seeing if he shifts.

"Do you have ants in your ass?" I hear his voice whispering through his morning rasp.

"You're squeezing me," I grumble.

"I did it to make you stop moving, you've been doing it for hours. I couldn't stand being kicked anymore, so I hugged you tightly. Seems like it calmed you down."

I could say it's a lie, but I know it's true. I'd forgotten that I have the terrible habit of moving a lot in my sleep. My sisters have mentioned it countless times, which is why they never shared a bed with me.

"You should have mentioned this before we went to sleep, I think I forgot..."

"You think so?" He was being ironic.

"Yes, I'm sure," I murmur.

"It would have been important to mention it. I was almost going to sleep on the couch," Abdul finally removes his arm from under me, doing the same with the one on top.

I miss his body, but now I have the chance to look at the ceiling and lie on my back, pulling the blanket up to my neck to keep him from seeing my nudity.

"Sorry, I can sleep in another room if necessary," I murmur in disgust.

"You won't! This bed will be yours for as long as I say."

"I thought my movements bothered you," I turn my face and look into his eyes, seeing him lying on his side.

"For your problem, I have a solution. It took me a while, but I figured out that squeezing you tightly is what calms you down."

I lie on my side, facing my husband, who has messy black hair.

"This seems so... so..." I can't find the right word to use, so I let the sentence die.

"So what?"

"Possessive?"

"Maybe," he adjusts the blanket, making my side fall down.

He did this on purpose, as his eyes soon fall on my breasts, a move that makes me pull the blanket back over my body.

"You know I've seen all this before, right?" he mocks.

"Different occasions," I refuse to give in.

"The occasion might change, but your body doesn't, unless you're carrying my child." He lets out a half-smile, making me swallow hard.

"Do you think I can get pregnant from just one time?" I ask curiously.

"Well, if you prefer, we can try again," His eyes sparkle.

"I think it's better if we wait."

"Why do you think that?"

"I don't want to lie with you knowing that you might be sharing the same bed with me and your mistress. Once is already enough humiliation. Does anyone else know about this?"

"No, no one knows. No one needs to know..."

"What will people think of me if someone finds out?" I let out a long sigh.

"What should they think of you?" Abdul keeps making me speak.

"That I'm not good enough? Everyone already thinks I'm naïve, a shadow of my aunt, especially with this..."

I turn as if to leave the bed, wanting to ignore this feeling of humiliation inside me. It's not enough to grow up knowing I'll have to obey a man; I also have to tolerate a mistress.

Just as I'm about to leave, Abdul pulls my arm, brings me back to the bed, and wraps a leg around each side of my waist, pinning me there.

"How about a deal?" he asks confidently.

His face hovering above mine examines every feature of my face.

"What are you talking about?" I ask.

"I'll be yours for this week, and in exchange, we'll have sex every night to increase the chance of having a child."

"What do I get out of it? A rented husband?" I let out a half-smile.

"Aren't you on board?" He furrows his brow.

"Do you really want a child so much?"

"Yes, I never wanted one because it was always indifferent to me, but now that we're married, I want it."

"If you want a child so much, it's good that it worked the first time we did the act..." I can't bring myself to say the word sex.

"You're not going to have sex with me anymore?" He tilts his head to the side.

"I was trained to serve my husband. I'll do that, I'll respect him, but as for infidelity, I'm not obligated to accept it." My words come out with resolve.

Abdul lets out a sideways smile as if he's mocking me.

"And here I thought you were a foolish girl with no personality. It seems I was wrong."

"We were both deceived..." I complete his sentence.

"So no deal?"

"There's no deal, there's a better possibility for you. And what about me? Can I do the same later?"

I think I shouldn't have said that. He quickly grabs my neck, not squeezing, but making a point.

"Never, understand? No one will lay a finger on you but me!" he growls, getting off me.

Abdul doesn't even care about being naked around the room. His body is tall, muscular, with a broad chest and few visible hairs. His member touches his stomach, still erect. Will it go back to normal?

"Don't you want to finish with my cock inside you?" he looks at me with angry eyes.

"No!"

"All this because of this nonsense?"

"Nonsense to you! It's important to me. It might have been good, but I lived 24 years without it; I can live more..."

"The problem is that now you've experienced it, you know what it is..."

"I want to know what it's like to have my husband all to myself." I sit on the bed "I accept that you have a second wife, but I won't accept a mistress. As long as she exists, you won't have me!"

"I already have her, and if it makes you feel any less proud, I can have you whenever and however I want. You're foolish and naïve; with a snap of my fingers, I'll fuck you, and you know what else?" I wait, looking at him, hoping he continues "You'll beg for more, moaning my name copiously!"

"Then try!" I tilt my chin defiantly.

Abdul huffs and goes into the bathroom.

If my father knew I was confronting my husband, he might punish me. This isn't what they taught me, but Abdul brings out even the quietest side of me. He makes me hate him and desire him with equal intensity.

CHAPTER SIX

Ayda

I enter the breakfast room with my husband, his unfriendly expression making it clear that he's irritated.

At the end of the table, I see the emir seated next to his wife.

"Hello, my son," Maya greets her child.

Abdul pulls out a chair for me to sit next to his mother, directly across from Malika, the emir's wife, sitting opposite her.

"Brother, I need you with me at the parliament today," Hassan calls Abdul's attention.

I sit down dejectedly next to Abdul and Maya.

"Join us, Sadira," I hear Hassan's commanding voice.

I briefly lift my face and meet the eyes of the third wife of Abdul's deceased father.

The woman sits down across from me.

"Thank you, dear," the woman with the dragging voice responds to the emir.

I don't know much about Sadira; she rarely visits the Zabeel palace. I didn't even see her at our wedding, which suggests she arrived this morning.

"How long do you plan to stay here, Sadi?" Maya asks the third wife.

"I don't know, I think I need a bit of excitement in my life..." I notice the woman's eyes linger on my husband.

She isn't an old woman; her marriage to his father was notable because she was younger than him. Sadira must be around 40 years old, nearly the same age as Abdul.

"It's a pity; the reason for the excitement left this palace," Elahe mocks, remembering her mother.

"Ah, that was chaos," Malika murmurs.

"Hurricane Zenda..." one of the brothers declares from the end of the table.

"Wow, how awful," Sadira says, filling her cup with tea "but now we have the girl she left behind."

Her smile towards me was somewhat forced.

"No, Ayda isn't like her aunt; from the little we've talked, she's the ideal wife for Abdul," Maya, my mother-in-law, defends me.

"Ah, I thought... sorry dear," Another one of those same smiles was directed at me.

I just nod without bothering to speak. I take a cup.

"Tea?" Abdul asks me.

"Yes, please..." I murmur.

He fills my cup. He serves some pastries and asks if I want more; there were several things on the table.

"This is fine," I whisper, my eyes widening as I see my plate full and he keeps offering me more food.

Abdul lowers his eyes and inspects my plate.

"You could eat more; it's still not enough," he raises his face to me, frowning.

"If I want to have a terrible stomachache later."

"Who told you to eat like a bird..."

"Like what I'm in the mood for," I raise an eyebrow.

"I see your marriage is calm, brother," Hassan interrupts my brief disagreement with my husband.

"If she plans to carry my child, she needs to eat better," Abdul gestures for me to start eating.

"Speaking like that, you remind me so much of Hakan. He said exactly the same thing when we got married," Sadira declares.

"Wow, that man knew how to control everyone around him," Maya murmurs with a sigh.

"Yes, I see a lot of him in Hassan and Abdul," Sadira sighs again as she mentions Abdul's name.

My husband huffs beside me, as if he didn't like that.

I decide to lower my face, eating in silence. I let them converse among themselves. I can hear some whispers directed at me; I know they're talking about me.

Abdul finishes eating first beside me.

"Do you need anything?" he asks in a whisper.

"No," I turn my face, meeting his eyes on mine.

He subtly raises his hand, adjusting my hijab to better cover my hair.

"There, that's better."

"Perfectionist," I murmur.

"Zealous," he shrugs, raising his eyes to his brother. "Ready?"

"Yes, let's go," Hassan replies.

The two men at the table stand up. The emir lifts his fingers and gently caresses his wife's cheek so subtly it's almost imperceptible.

He doesn't show emotions often, but when it comes to his wife, he breaks some protocols. One of them is showing affection in front of others.

"If you need anything, send me a message," he whispers to her, making sure those closest can hear.

Abdul says nothing, just leaves with his brother, both in white robes.

As soon as the emir leaves the table, many follow, leaving only my mother-in-law beside me, Sadira and Malika in front of me.

"I see my son is treating you well," Maya affirms beside me.

"Yes..." I murmur, unsure of what to say.

"I'm glad you married him. I was almost thinking my son would never get married," my mother-in-law continues.

"I suppose I'm happy he chose me," I furrow my brow, unsure if that's the best way to speak to my mother-in-law.

"But we know he only took this step because Hassan ordered him to," Sadira interrupts us.

"How do you know?" Malika gracefully wipes her mouth with a napkin and asks. "I ask because not many people know; they made this decision among themselves, and you don't live here."

"Ah..." the woman is caught off guard, and I'm curious. "News travels fast; Habbib told me. He's here at the palace almost every day."

Sadira stumbles over her words, clearly uncomfortable with the direct comments from the emirate princess.

"Hassan ordered it, but he always left the option open for his brother, so if he married Ayda, it was because he wanted to. Of course, there was some pressure from his brother, but my husband knows what he's doing. If Abdul and Ayda are together, it's because Allah willed it; nothing happens by chance..." Malika defends me again. This woman literally has no filter.

She doesn't feel intimidated; she's the type of woman who stands up to defend those by her side. Am I on that same side?

"Sorry if I offended you," Sadira turns her attention back to me.

"I'm fine," I blink a few times.

"I'm going to the mall; do you want to come with me?" Malika stands up, asking me.

"Go ahead, dear, it's good for you two to be friends..." Maya answers for me, and I agree.

CHAPTER SEVEN

Ayda

"Shall we go to that store?" Malika asks as she walks beside me. She gives a nod, which makes me notice the lingerie store.

"Can we?" I whisper, curious.

"What's stopping us?" She turns her face towards me, her beautiful green eyes sparkling.

"Those men following us?" I raise an eyebrow.

A few steps away, we are being followed by security guards.

"Oh, them, don't worry, they won't come in with us. They might be brutes, but they know how to give us privacy. Come on..."

Malika takes my hand and leads me into the store.

We are soon recognized and attended to, with Malika, being a good princess, promptly asking to see what she wanted.

"Could we be alone, please?" Mali asks the saleswoman as soon as the woman guides us to the section she wanted.

I walk past the racks, where many lingerie pieces are hanging on hangers.

Malika stands in front of me on the other side of the rack.

"The last time I was at the mall with Maya, I asked to go into this store, and she didn't want to. Well, that was the day Zenda overheard Khalil's conversation..." she trails off, lost in her thoughts.

"I'm sorry, I never wanted to marry Hassan, Aunt Zenda was always the greedy one," I murmur.

"I know that, but if I may offer an opinion..." I listen closely to what she has to say. "I haven't lived with Hassan for long, but if there's one thing I've learned in that family, it's not to stay silent because some people can swallow you alive. I'm not talking about your husband..."

"Are you saying this because of what everyone says about me? Without an opinion?" I whisper, watching her run her fingers over the lingerie.

"Yes, that too..."

"My parents were so strict, and now that I'm away from them, I feel lost, directionless, and unsure of where to go," we look at each other for a long moment.

"I know this is a matter of time, but you could start speaking a little louder. You're always whispering, and often we can't even hear what you're saying."

"Like this? Like this?" I speak in a slightly louder tone, finding my voice strange.

She smiles, nodding her head.

"For a start, it's perfect."

"Can I ask you something?" I ask as she nods. "What did Abdul say about this marriage? Be honest."

Malika remains silent for a long time, looking at the various pieces of lingerie.

"He didn't want this union, which is no news to you. He always complained that you were a shadow of Zenda since she was always by his side."

"Did Abdul never say why he was never interested in another woman?" I ask, curious.

"Not to me, and I don't believe even to my husband. Can I ask you something?" I nod, waiting for her to continue. "Have you consummated the marriage?"

Malika is direct, and I admit I felt my face flush.

"Yes, we have," I confirm, my embarrassment clear as I talk about the subject.

"And, um... was it good?" The emir's wife seems quite curious.

"Yes, uncomfortable, to be honest, a bit painful," I look around to confirm we are still alone.

"But there's still something bothering you," she seems to read my thoughts.

"Yes, there is, but I don't know if I should talk about it," I let a weak smile escape my lips.

"I don't know what it is, but if you want to share, I promise I can keep a secret."

"Even from your husband?" Perhaps sharing this with someone might be good for a new perspective on what I should do.

"Even from Hassan, if necessary," she whispers, somewhat curious.

I take a deep breath, considering whether or not to speak. After all, my husband said that no one knows about this and he never even considered telling anyone.

I exhale forcefully, trusting the woman in front of me and tell her what I know:

"Abdul has a mistress..."

"What?" Malika doesn't let me continue, interrupting me in a loud whisper.

"Yes, that's right. He had the audacity to tell me he has a mistress and said we would only have one night together, just an act to consummate the marriage, but his subsequent behavior left me confused," I murmur, looking around.

"What happened next?" Malika leans over the rack to listen better.

"He said he wanted another week, that one time isn't enough to get pregnant, but that's not what he said at the beginning."

His conversation still confuses me.

"And what did you say? Don't tell me you gave in to him?" The woman in front of me frowns, her eyes narrowing.

"I didn't give in. He has a mistress! I felt humiliated, like I was being replaced. How dare he have me as a wife and reveal that he has a mistress?"

"By Allah, you made the right choice. If there's one thing I've learned about the men in this family, it's that the more you stand firm, the more they give in."

"But will he go after her? Am I just the second option, the front-wife?" I deflate at my words.

"No, Ayda, he won't go after her. Not as long as you hold the reins. But who is this mistress?"

"He didn't say, just mentioned that she's someone he can't acknowledge..."

We both fall silent, contemplating the possibilities around us.

"Well, let's stay alert to all the signs. I promise I won't tell Hassan, but we need to take some action regarding Abdul. I might like him a lot—he's the most fun in the palace—but a mistress? That's too much, even for him."

Malika was as outraged as I was.

"What do you have in mind?" I ask, curious.

"Hassan loves to see me wearing daring lingerie, which is why we're here. We'll buy some for you too," she lets a sly smile escape her lips.

"Abdul told me he wants me to sleep without clothes," I ask, confused.

"Abdul doesn't have control over you, though we know he thinks he does. But behind closed doors, we can control them. Just know how to use that to your advantage. Don't sleep without clothes; always wear the outfits we'll buy today, revealing just enough to drive him crazy. Ah, I love driving my husband wild," Malika lets out a little grin.

The emir's wife helped me pick out many sets, and we spent the day shopping.

CHAPTER EIGHT

Ayda

After dinner, we all gather in the lounge. Malika is next to her husband, smiling as she whispers something to him.

I decide to sit in a secluded corner. I've always been good at observing everything around me. Elahe is sitting in an armchair, holding a book and lost in thought.

Abdul joins the group, sitting next to his mother. He doesn't even bother to look for me. I see his eyes settle on Sadira, who is entering the room and then sits next to him.

She smiles at him.

"How was your day at the mall?" Maya asks Malika.

"And I thought you were only going to one store," Elahe closes her book and joins the conversation.

"We were going to, but I ended up dragging Ayda along to several stores. Time flew by so quickly that, before we knew it, it was late," Malika declares loudly.

"Letting the princess loose in a mall is like leaving a child in an amusement park. Should I really make her rest because of the pregnancy?" Hassan complains affectionately.

Sometimes I wonder if Abdul will also call me his princess now that we are married.

"My Sheikh, my pregnancy is going well; I don't want to stop anything because of it. You can be at ease," she speaks tenderly.

"Did you buy anything for me?" Elahe asks, pouting.

"Yes, we asked to have it left in your room. Take a look later,"

"Ah..." she claps her hands, "I love being pampered."

"I hope your husband does the same for you," Hassan murmurs to his sister with disdain.

Hassan has never been very supportive of his sister's engagement to the Sheikh of Agu Dhami.

"And you, dear Ayda, did you enjoy it?" Maya asks me to include me in the conversation, drawing everyone's attention to me.

I look towards Malika and try to practice my voice a little louder, remembering what she told me during our outing.

"It was nice; I haven't had so much fun in a while," I blink a few times, smiling at my mother-in-law.

My voice comes out a little louder, maybe at a normal volume for anyone else, but not for me, as I've always spoken softly.

"Now I'm envious," Elahe makes a bit of a drama to shift the focus from my change in tone.

"What's stopping you from going to another emirate?" Hassan says to his sister, who sticks out her tongue at him.

"It's a good kind of envy; it's nice to know you're not fighting, so I don't have to call for help," Elahe crinkles her nose as she always does to show indifference.

My cousin has always been realistic and knows her place in the family, though she's a bit of a dreamer.

I don't say anything, just stay quietly in my corner observing everything, unsure how to fit into this large family, even though I'm Elahe's cousin. She's the only one from my family left here in the palace, as her siblings, who are my cousins and Zenda's children, have all moved in with her.

I raise my eyes to Abdul, who keeps his attention on me. He doesn't show any interest in the two women beside him. Sadira continues talking next to him incessantly, but Maya is the one answering her questions.

I wonder why Sadira decided to visit the family now, when it's clear she never comes to the Zabeel palace to stay overnight.

"If you'll excuse me," I ask, getting up from the cushion where I'm sitting.

Since I spoke softly, no one noticed. I don't think even my husband noticed, as he's currently focused on what Sadira is saying to him.

I squint, noticing that she whispers something to him that makes him clench his jaw.

In the midst of my movement, I catch Malika's eye, who looks in my direction, winking and making it clear that she'll be keeping an eye on everything.

"Good night, everyone," I murmur so they won't say I didn't say goodbye.

Perhaps spending the day at the mall with Malika has become tiring. I wonder how she manages it, especially being pregnant.

It makes me think that I might also be pregnant. Is that what I want, to get pregnant right away with my husband?

I climb the stairs, reflecting on my movements and how strange it is to live in such a large palace, filled with people, and at the same time, feel so lonely.

Aunt Zenda made her reputation here, and since I was always following her around, it reflected on me. All because she wanted the ruler, Malika's husband, to take me as his second wife.

Knowing that it was Abdul who made the request seemed like the right choice at the time, since he was single and wouldn't be a new wife in the middle of an existing union.

It all seemed too easy, especially since Abdul revealed his true intentions. A lover—this still hasn't sunk in.

I enter my room, or rather, my husband's room. I don't know when he'll send me to another room, since I am his only wife. If he wants, he can keep me here, and we won't need a second room. Just like the emir and his princess, who use the same quarters.

I close the door behind me and go straight to the closet.

I scan the hangers and find the various pieces I bought with Mali, satin nightgowns in every color and style.

Should I do what she suggested?

Go against my husband's request?

He asked for me to be nude. Wearing this, I'll be, theoretically, semi-nude.

I might end up making Abdul more irritated.

And maybe, just maybe, I'll enjoy the effect it has on me. So, I decide to put on one of the nightgowns I bought with Mali. I walk to the colorful fabrics and choose a baby blue one. I take off my tunic and put it in the laundry basket. I put on the lingerie that is part of the set and see how well it fits my body. Lastly, I put on the nightgown.

I leave my hair loose and head toward the bed.

I fluff the pillow and pull down the blanket.

I'm about to lie down when the door opens and reveals my husband.

CHAPTER NINE

Ayda

"What are you doing?" he asks as he locks the door behind him. "Going to sleep?" I whisper.

"What was our agreement?"

"Your agreement?" I raise an eyebrow.

"Whatever, I don't want you in clothes, even if they look marvelous on you," Abdul continues walking towards me.

"We're just going to sleep. What difference will it make?"

"It will change everything. Take it off now, Ayda," he commands with a serious voice.

I huff; in theory, it seemed so easy.

"What will happen if I don't take it off?" I bite the corner of my lip.

"I'll rip these damn pieces," his eyes scan my body.

Abdul stops and stands in front of me. I gently arch my face and observe his serious features, with his thick beard marking his face.

Seeing my lack of movement, Abdul grabs the collar of my nightgown.

"I'll take it off," I murmur, trying to stop him.

"Too late..." he doesn't even finish speaking before he starts tearing the nightgown.

The thin fabric tears in half under my husband's large hands, uncaring of my wide eyes.

He drops the piece to the floor and looks at my lace bra.

Holding my waist, he turns my body and unfastens my bra, which falls to the ground.

I am in a trance, not knowing what to do, trying to find the strength to resist my husband.

I feel his hand on my neck, pushing my hair to the side, exposing my skin, and soon his hand is replaced by his lips. He kisses my burning skin, making my treacherous body shiver at his touch.

My husband's hands embrace me from behind, and I can feel his member brushing against my buttocks through his tunic.

"I need to fuck this little pussy," he murmurs into my neck, knowing that I am about to surrender to him.

I close my eyes at his dirty words and feel the masculine essence of his scent, I want, I crave his touches.

But I remember that obstacle...

I open my eyes immediately and stare at the bedroom wall, catching my husband off guard when I take a step away from him, turning my trembling legs towards him, covering my breasts in my embarrassment for almost giving in like a fool.

"Are you crazy?" he asks through gritted teeth.

"Crazy is you for thinking I have a short memory," I murmur, trying to find my voice, still feeling the tingles from his hands where they had touched.

"Why be so foolish, when you want this too?" he huffs, clearly frustrated.

"As the saying goes, wanting is not the same as being able."

"I want you, Ayda," he practically roars.

I lower my eyes down his body, seeing his member lightly pressing against his white tunic.

I let out a long sigh through my slightly open mouth.

"Admit that you want me, Ayda..."

"I want you, husband," I whisper, lifting my curious eyes to his body, stopping at his face—"but my stance regarding your respect remains the same."

"You can't forget that, can you?" I can see the moment he clenches his fists.

"No, I can't forget."

"Okay!"

He whispers and turns his back to me, heading towards the door he opened and leaving our room.

I stay there alone, my eyes clouding and filling with tears.

Where did he go? Is his lover from this palace?

I turn my body, sit on the bed, and lay my head on the pillow. I curl up on my side and let the tears fall. Abdul wanted me to warm his arms, and I rejected him. Now he has sought comfort in other arms.

Something inside me screams, making it clear that I shouldn't feel guilty. I demanded the minimum from my husband, and he cannot give it to me.

I close my eyes trying to fall asleep, losing myself in the pain of my broken heart. I can hear my parents' voices pounding in my mind. *"If only you had given in to him, this wouldn't have happened."*

I am absolutely sure that's what they would say in favor of the good union I have. This is an advantageous marriage with a Sheikh, the brother of the ruler, which will make my future children Sheiks, not mere mortals like us. This marriage makes me a Sheikh's princess.

I take a deep breath, the tears that once flowed copiously now cease.

I try to pull from my memory any instance of Abdul with another woman, wondering who could be so forbidden to him that they wouldn't have a relationship. Or does he want this woman only for his pleasure? But... all of this without ever wanting a serious commitment with another woman?

I know better than anyone that this union was only made because of Hassan, who demanded that his brother marry, after all, Abdul is already 37 years old. At this age, his father already had two wives and many children.

I focus again on my husband and the hints about his lover. Only one person comes to mind: Sadira, who appeared out of nowhere, a day after our union, wanting to give too much advice.

Everything starts to make sense. He went after her. My whole body recoils; he went to her arms. *By Allah.*

My eyes fill with tears again, tears of anger. What did I do to deserve such betrayal?

I hear the door to the room open, luckily, it is still dark. I smell his perfume, so I know it's him. His feet drag silently on the floor.

I stay still and thank, as the tears have stopped once again.

The light from the bedside lamp is turned on, and the dim light hits my closed eyelids, tormenting me as my face is stained with tears.

"Open your eyes," he practically orders.

Releasing a long sigh, I open my eyes and find his inscrutable expression.

"Why were you crying?" he asks, tilting his head to the side and crossing his arms.

"Because I hate you," I whisper, my voice choked.

Abdul takes a deep breath, as if thinking about what he should say. He doesn't say anything, turns off the lamp again, and the room is dark once more.

"Try to sleep; I'm going to bathe," he whispers. "I don't have a lover anymore."

He declares it so quietly that I'm not sure if that's what I heard.

CHAPTER TEN

Ayda

I try to stay awake after what Abdul said, but it was impossible; it almost seemed like that was what I needed to fall asleep.

I squeeze my eyelids shut, but the light makes me open my eyes, and I realize the day has already broken.

I take a deep breath and notice that I am alone in the room. I turn my body, but the bed beside me is empty. Where is he? Did he sleep here?

I run my hand through my hair and sit up on the bed.

I lift my face and hear the door being opened. I see Malika peek her head inside.

"Ah, I'm glad you're awake," she says. "Good morning..."

"Come in," I murmur, pulling the sheet around my neck. "Did something happen?" I ask as she enters the room.

"Nothing, no..." Malika lets the sentence trail off as she looks around the room. "Abdul asked me to come get you. He left early with Hassan, Elahe, and Sadira. It seems they went to look at some horses."

The woman shrugs nonchalantly.

"Sadira too?" I ask, raising an eyebrow.

"Yes, why?" Malika seems puzzled by my reaction.

"Nothing, I guess it must just be in my head," I shake my head.

"What did you think?" The woman in front of me seems somewhat curious.

"Sometimes I think Sadira seems to be Abdul's lover, but that must be crazy..." She interrupts me.

"I thought I was the only one who came to that conclusion. Out of nowhere, she returned to our palace, trying to meddle in Abdul's life, playing the kind-hearted woman..."

"Unlike Aunt Zenda, who always showed her claws, she acts innocent," I murmur, completing Malika's line of thought.

"I think we need to stay alert about her," Mali sighs thoughtfully.

"Abdul revealed something yesterday—I needed to confide in someone about what he told me."

"I'm all ears; I promise my mouth is a tomb," the woman sits at the foot of the still messy bed.

"He told me he doesn't have a lover anymore, but he didn't go into details. He just revealed it and went to take a shower. I was so tired that I couldn't talk to him."

"So, does that mean he's already being won over by you?" she opens her mouth in a small *Oh*.

"I don't know; I don't even know why he told me that."

"It's pretty obvious. He wants you and is renouncing the other to be with you," Mali releases a long sigh.

"This is madness; it doesn't make sense, not after everything he told me," I shake my head, even more confused.

"Your head is almost smoking. Forget about it; let's go downstairs to eat," Malika stands up.

I know I'm still in my nightgown, so she gave me privacy and left the room.

I enter the *closet*, choose one of my favorite tunics in red tones, which contrasts with my almond-shaped eyes and makes my skin appear naturally tanned. Even though I'm always covered by fabrics, I have a subtle cocoa tone.

I pass by the bathroom, wash my face, and braid the side of my shoulder to keep my hair more hidden when I wear my *hijab*.

After finishing in the bathroom, I come out, take the red *hijab* fabric from the bed where I had left it, and place it on my head.

I leave the room and find Malika fiddling with her phone, a broad smile on her lips. I release a long sigh, making her notice my presence.

"Ah, let's go downstairs; you must be hungry," Mali gestures for us to go down together.

"When you came to live here, how did you deal with missing your home?" I ask in a low voice.

She needed me to repeat the question because she hadn't heard, and I repeated it, listening to her answer:

"At first, it was hard. After all, I never wanted to give in to my husband, but in the end, everything worked out. I think I spent two days at my parents' house, away from my husband, and it was worse than if it were the other way around, me being with him. That was the peak of our madness to realize that we were made for each other. Do you miss home?" she directs the question to me.

"It's not really missing; after all, everything was so regulated there, you couldn't do this, you couldn't do that," I mimic my father's way of speaking. "I was raised to serve a husband, but I wasn't prepared for this, a husband who has a lover. With all this surrounding me, this crazy desire for him to touch me, to accept me as I am..." My sentence trails off, allowing me to sigh as I remember my husband.

"I know exactly how that feels; after all, I went through something similar. But if you take my advice, which isn't from a superprotective and controlling father: don't give in to your husband's wants. If you do that now, it becomes a frequent habit. I always wanted my husband's love, and I pursued it until the end, and I succeeded. I have a husband who is only mine, someone who honors and respects me."

We enter the breakfast room, where I sit facing Malika.

"Well, I've already eaten, but since I'm eating for two, I'll join you. This palace feels so lonely; it seems like everyone decided to go out. Even Maya went out to visit her daughters."

I smile in gratitude to Malika for staying with me, so I don't feel so alone.

I spend the day with Malika, we walk around the palace and explore places even she hadn't been to.

It's ridiculously large; we even got lost in one of the wings! Luckily, we were rescued by one of the staff members passing by at the time.

The lack of news from Abdul starts to make me even more anxious. Perhaps with Elahe there, they wouldn't do anything that could expose them. Why is this whole situation making me feel this way? There are so many whys, but no answers.

In the middle of the afternoon, I sit with Malika in the afternoon tea room with a small table between us. A lady serves us tea in small cups, and I cross my feet while keeping my back straight.

Mali was distracted by her phone until she looked up at me and spoke.

"Elahe asked where we are..." She doesn't get to finish her sentence before the girl walks through the door.

"There you are..." My cousin enters the room with a smile "Mali, Hassan asked that, when you're finished here, you meet him in your room."

She gives a suggestive smile.

"Alright, but you might want to wipe that smile off your lips," Mali raises her hand toward her mouth.

"Sadira got sick during the trip, so Abdul accompanied her to her quarters..."

"Oh, really?" I don't wait for her to finish speaking; I immediately get up. "Where is her room? I'm worried."

I pretend to be concerned about the woman's health because I need to see with my own eyes to draw conclusions about my suspicions.

CHAPTER ELEVEN

Abdul

I climb the last few steps with Sadira by my side. It seems that nothing I said to her the previous night had any effect. Here she is, finding an excuse for us to be alone.

"We need to talk..." she says as we approach her room.

The place is more private and there's no one around, so she immediately grabs my hand and pulls me into her room.

"We have nothing more to discuss. I was clear with you, I made it very explicit, I don't want any more..."

"And what about our oath? You promised you would take care of me," she tries to hold my other hand, which I pull away, keeping a good distance from her.

"I didn't say I would stop taking care of you, I just don't want any more secret meetings. I realized that being married makes it more risky, so it's better if we don't meet anymore," I say softly so only she can hear, constantly glancing at the open door.

Of course, all of this is a lie. I want Ayda, damn it, how I want her.

I've never desired a woman in my bed as much as I desire my wife. Everything about her fascinates me. She doesn't even seem like the same shy, downcast girl who used to frequent the palace, always obeying her aunt's orders. Behind those layers of fabric is a woman who is incredibly desirable, and, by Allah, just closing my eyes, I can hear her sighs.

"You'll get tired of her..."

"Sadira, understand, it's risky. You being here is risky," I emphasize more than once. "Why did you come to this palace, after all?"

"Why else? I missed my family..."

"Honestly," I huff without letting her finish her sentence, "I sincerely ask you to go back to your home. We will not resume our affair..."

"So, I'll tell your brother. What do you think he'll think?" The woman crosses her arms. "We know how much he values family and the innocence of his father's wives, to whom he was very loyal."

"I wouldn't dare do such a thing," I murmur, taking small steps towards her.

"Oh, dear Abdul, I would dare. I want you, I haven't grown tired of having you in my bed," a victorious smile appears on her lips.

"Then go back to your home," I let out a long sigh, realizing I'm in a terrible bind.

"I'll only go under one condition," Sadira holds onto the hem of her hijab.

"And what would that be?" I ask, apprehensive about the answer.

"Now, you and I on this bed to enjoy the few minutes of peace we have," the woman bites her lip. She knows how much I love hot sex and is aware of all my tastes in bed.

I look over her shoulder at the neatly made bed and know it wouldn't be a sacrifice for my body to surrender to that moment.

However, the only thing that comes to mind is the brown eyes of my wife, as I saw them last night, with sadness etched in them.

Damn it! I shouldn't care about Ayda, I shouldn't care if she's happy or sad, but I do care. She's the only one I'm thinking about.

"Abdul, do you want me to tell your brother?" The woman in front of me presses her body against mine, pulling me out of my reverie.

"No! Hassan can't know about this," I murmur, determined.

I know I'll have to go to bed with her and that, once again, I'll lie to my wife.

This should be easy. But it's not!

"I'll close the door," I whisper, moving away from my mistress, whom I wanted to keep away, but fate insists on bringing her back. What a hell of confusion!

With determined steps, I grip the doorknob, not before noticing a movement outside. I frown, puzzled.

I walk out of the room. I would recognize that silhouette anywhere. Even from behind, I know it was her.

Ayda, walking in the opposite direction, I know she clearly heard my conversation with Sadira.

Could it get any worse? Obviously, it could!

Ayda heard, Ayda now knows who my mistress is, and worse, she knows that I lied. Damn it! A thousand times damn it!

I run my hand through my hair, almost pulling it out from the pressure I'm under.

"This will have to wait..." My words trail off.

I don't hear what Sadira says, I just run after my wife, who I lost sight of. She can't have gone far. I start opening doors as I go through the corridors. I was almost losing hope when I open a door so abruptly that it crashes against the wall.

I raise my face and see her silhouette standing in front of a window. The room is completely empty; it must be another one of the countless rooms in this palace that serve no purpose.

I enter, close the door behind me, and soon hear her voice.

"So she's your mistress," her voice is hoarse.

"Yes," I murmur, catching my breath.

"I suspected as much," I can hear a forced laugh escape her lips.

"I... I..." For the first time, I am at a loss for words.

Ayda turns her body and her disappointed eyes towards me.

"And I even believed what you told me last night. What a fool I was!" My wife bites her lip, and I can see it has turned white from the pressure she applied.

Her eyes start to well up as if she is struggling not to cry.

"And it was true, but it's complicated," I walk slowly towards her.

"Complicate it then, because I don't understand. What's wrong with me, Abdul? What?" Ayda shakes her head.

I want to go to her, to embrace her, to hold her in my arms and lose myself in her sweet, innocent lips. Damn it!

This woman is completely untouched; only I have seen her naked, only I have kissed her. How can I not be completely crazy about her when everything about her is enticingly delicious?

"There's nothing wrong with you..."

"Then why her?" Ayda cuts me off, a tear falling down her delicate face.

Seeing her like this irritates me, and knowing that the reason she is like this is my fault irritates me even more.

Sadira needs to stop this. How can I hurt the purest woman I have ever known? Her pain is tearing me apart inside.

"It's complicated, Ayda, you would never understand..."

"I saw you walking towards the door, you were going to close it. Do you prefer her over your wife?" I don't answer immediately, knowing she will always be my preference.

But Sadira is blackmailing me. Sadira intends to tell my brother about our affair.

"Your silence answered my question..." she sighs in the middle of her speech.

"No, my silence didn't answer a damn thing!" I walk towards her.

Ayda sidesteps and quickly heads towards the door.

"I don't want to talk to you, I don't want to hear your excuses, just leave me alone."

I don't have time to chase after her, as she left the room as quickly as she walked to the door, leaving me there, alone with my damn thoughts. Maybe all this will be resolved if I talk to my brother myself.

He will probably kill me, but at least this revelation will come from my own mouth.

CHAPTER TWELVE

Ayda

The truth is, I didn't want to run into Abdul, not after hearing him fall into Sadira's trap, not after he didn't even consider the possibility that his actions could hurt me.

He prefers to stay with the mistress rather than tell his brother?

If only I could go back to my home, but that's impossible. If my father suspects that my marriage isn't going well, he might disown me, cast me out to the streets of bitterness. Where am I to run?

I let out a long sigh. Maybe spending the afternoon with Malika exploring the palace had some result. Now I know where to hide. I've lost track of time, not knowing how long I've been standing in front of this window.

I sat on the windowsill to look out at the back of the palace. I believe no one passes by there often, as it is literally in the dark.

In the distance, I see the sun giving way to night. I bite my lip, tired from crying. I'm tired of not being accepted, because, in the end, he preferred her. Instead of me, he preferred her.

The mistress! Instead of the wife who might be carrying his child in her womb.

Footsteps echoing on the floor are heard outside the door.

"Ayda?" Malika's voice is present "Where are you?"

I let out a long sigh and, jumping from the window, head towards the door I had opened, spotting the girl looking for me.

"I'm here," I murmur.

"Oh, finally! I don't know what happened, but you need to come downstairs. Your parents have just arrived..."

"What? How?" I stammer, my eyes wide, interrupting her.

"Yes, they arrived unexpectedly. Hassan and Abdul are in the sitting room with them," Malika grabs my hand "Can you see them? You look terrible."

"Can you? Is my face very swollen?" I ask as we descend several flights of stairs.

Crossing a few corridors since I was far away.

"How did you find me?" I ask, confused.

"When we were here this afternoon, you said you liked the calmness of this place, so it was the first place I came to look for you. Abdul had volunteered to search for you, but seeing his impatience, I realized something had happened, so I told him to stay and welcome your parents."

"Thank you," I murmur.

"On a scale from one to ten, how bad is your relationship with Abdul?"

"At the moment, I'd say about an eight," I sigh and stop walking, catching my breath. I ask Malika to check my face to see if I look presentable to meet my parents.

"Now you look fine," Malika tucks a strand of hair into my hijab, smiling and trying to reassure me "I know your situation with Abdul isn't the best, but try not to let it show in front of your parents."

I nod, walking towards the door where I would meet my parents.

Taking a deep breath, I exhale slowly and put a smile on my face as I enter the room. My eyes quickly meet my father's.

He is sitting next to my mother, his eyes fixed on me as if trying to uncover if I'm hiding something.

"Dad, Mom, what a surprise!" I walk towards them, keeping the smile on my lips, hugging each of them.

Not without first hearing my father's whisper in my ear, "Behave, Ayda, why speak so loudly? Don't forget you have an image to uphold," and there went all my freedom, always with someone wanting to control my life wherever I looked.

I scan the room and find an empty spot next to my husband. I had to swallow hard to walk towards him.

Without looking directly into his eyes, I sit beside him, my leg brushing against his gently.

"You arrived just in time, we will be having dinner soon, and I hope to have your company as our guests," Hassan says in a pleasant tone as the head of the palace.

My husband remains silent beside me.

"Thank you for the invitation, Emir. We just came to visit our daughter and see if she is being a good wife," Esmail finishes speaking, turning his gaze towards my husband.

We are seated across from my parents while Hassan is seated in an armchair with Malika beside him.

"There was no need to ask that, Ayda is an excellent companion and a great wife," Abdul lies shamelessly.

"That's why we invested in the best education for her," my father says proudly as always.

I lower my face in embarrassment at the awkward situation.

"I'm sure of it," Abdul declares.

The door to the room opens, and at that moment, I lift my face to see who is entering. I have to swallow hard when I see the woman walk through the door; it's Sadira, alongside Maya. My mother-in-law who doesn't know the viper beside her.

I flinch when, suddenly, Abdul intertwines his fingers with mine. He tries to calm me, but it has no effect.

"What a pleasure to have you here with us," Maya quickly recognizes my parents and introduces them to Sadira.

The woman, in her most insincere manner, greets my parents and says:
"Your daughter is a little darling, made to be the princess of a Sheikh."

I snort quietly and my eyes fix on my husband's hand intertwined with mine, a gesture that could be noticed by everyone present, even my parents, who frequently direct their attention there.

"Tonight I'll explain everything to you," Abdul murmurs close to my ear, making me turn my face slowly to look into his eyes.

"Stay and have dinner with us," Hassan repeats his invitation as soon as dinner is served.

My parents end up accepting. Mom walks beside me and whispers how proud they are of my marriage and that I should continue obeying my husband.

Little do they know that I am exactly at odds with my husband.

At least dinner goes well. I sit as far away from Sadira as possible, keeping myself distant from her sweet talk that no longer deceives me.

CHAPTER THIRTEEN

Ayda

I say goodbye to my parents and hug each of them. The dinner was calm, and throughout the evening, I avoided my father's accusing gaze, which is why I received a reprimand from him during the farewell hug.

I let out a long sigh; it seems like lately, all I can do is swallow everything in silence.

On one side, I have my controlling parents, and on the other, my husband, who, above all, has a mistress.

Esmail and Raja leave, promising to visit us again.

"It's late; I'll retire for the night," Sadira declares loudly in the room for everyone to hear.

I fix my gaze on her and notice she's paying attention to my husband.

Quickly, I turn my head, but Abdul is distracted, not even noticing that it was a hint directed at him. My husband has his head down while reading something on his phone. His thick black hair is messy.

I'm extremely angry with him, but I don't want to give Sadira the satisfaction of victory, even if it means locking Abdul in our room tonight, locking the door, and throwing away the key.

In the midst of my jealousy outburst, I end up saying:

"My Sheikh," I call my husband's attention, who quickly lifts his eyes from his phone. My voice is low, but what I say can be heard by everyone in the room—"today has been exhausting; why don't you accompany me to our room?"

Abdul's eyes widen, unsure if this is a trap or if I'm losing my mind.

I finish speaking and turn my face. I see Malika's amused expression, who must have picked up on what I was trying to do.

My husband, still suspicious, gets up from the sofa and walks towards me with a furrowed brow while I wait for him standing by the door.

I cross my arms and raise an eyebrow as I stare at Sadira, as if challenging her with my gaze. If she thinks she's dealing with an innocent and foolish girl, she is sorely mistaken.

I turn my back, knowing that Abdul is following me. I say nothing. With each step I climb, I can hear his breath behind me. When I devised this plan, it seemed easier. And now, what will I do?

We reach our room. I open the door, go in first, and see my husband follow me in.

"I'm trying to understand what's going on in your head," my husband immediately asks as I close the door.

Without responding immediately, I close the door, lock it, and take out the key. He didn't notice, but I've tucked the key into the pocket of my tunic. Abdul is only leaving this room over my dead body!

"At this moment?" I turn my body towards the bathroom—"nothing's going on..."

I shuffle my feet and enter the suite, closing the door behind me, but not before turning the key.

A victorious smile appears on my lips. How I would love to see him try to leave the room.

I remove my hijab, then the tunic, and leave the door key on the sink. I undo my hair braid and turn on the shower to step under the water. I let it fall over my body, helping me relax and think about my next steps while I lather up.

After the shower, I grab a robe from the counter, unsure of what to do next. Perhaps all my self-control is going out the window.

I dry my hair with a towel, brush it, but leave it damp. I wipe the mirror, clearing the steam. Staring at my reflection for several long seconds, I wonder what I should do.

I take a deep breath, pick up the key from the sink, and tuck it into the pocket of my robe.

Gathering all the courage I have left, I turn my back and leave the bathroom.

I open the door, look around for my husband until I see the balcony curtains moving and him coming from outside.

"Where's the key to the door?" he asks, walking slowly towards me.

"You want to leave?" I ask in a faint voice.

"If I asked where the key is, it's because I want to know."

"I don't know where it is," I shrug, lying with the utmost sincerity.

"There are only two people in this room. I didn't take the key, so it must be with you. Don't play dumb," Abdul keeps walking, and with each step he takes towards me, I take another step back.

I retreat into the bathroom, with the door open behind me. My body bumps into the counter, and I widen my eyes.

"Why, do you want the key?" My voice comes out softly.

"I don't owe you any explanations," he replies, lowering his face and stopping in front of me.

"Do you want to meet with her?" I question.

"I repeat, I don't owe you any explanations," he clenches his jaw tightly, and I can see how he tenses it.

"And... so, I don't know where the key is," I stammer, refusing to hand over the key that's in my pocket.

"The foolish girl, thinks she has some control over me?" At that moment, he was quicker, slipping his hand into the pocket of my robe and grabbing the key.

Damn!

In the midst of my impulse to grip his wrist, my movement makes the robe shift, revealing half of my breast, an act noticed by Abdul, who lowers his eyes and studies it for a long moment before pulling his arm away and leaving the bathroom, leaving me alone.

I walk towards him and ask:

"Why, Abdul, why are you going after her?" My voice comes out more anguished than I expected.

Tightening my robe around me, I hide my body.

"I'm not going after her..."

"You're lying, I don't believe it!" I don't let him finish speaking.

"That's why I told you I don't owe you an explanation of where I'm going," Abdul puts the key in the door handle.

"If you leave through that door..." My sentence dies with his intense gaze on me.

"What will happen?" My husband stops turning the key in the process of opening the door.

I bite my lip, knowing this was my only alternative. And if he renounces me anyway?

"If you leave through that door..." My courage doesn't go beyond that.

"And if I make you a proposal?" Abdul turns around to face me.

"And what would that be?"

"Be mine and I won't seek another; be mine for all the nights I'll face my brother, telling him the whole truth. But in return, be mine..." he stops speaking, looking at the empty bed.

I go back to biting my lip, unsure of what to do but knowing that I want him above all else.

CHAPTER FOURTEEN

Ayda

Abdul waited for my response, and it would have come if I hadn't felt dizzy, searching for something to hold onto before falling to the ground. With the impact, I hit my head on the floor.

"Ayda..." Abdul calls my name and comes towards me.

I blink several times. My husband picks me up and carries me to our bed, where he lays me down. He immediately takes out his phone, and I know he'll make a call.

"No," I say, trying to sit up, but he prevents me from doing so.

"I'm going to call the family doctor..."

"It's not necessary, it was just a dizziness," I cut him off because I don't want him to make the call.

"Dizziness isn't normal," In a moment of distraction, I stretch out my hand and grab the phone.

"In my case, it is. Since we got married, I've been on this roller coaster of ups and downs. I'm struggling to deal with these feelings; it shouldn't be like this..." I murmur, closing my eyes, relaxing my body, knowing that even he can't handle all this madness we're living. I can hear him let out a sigh before he starts talking again.

"I was going to talk to my brother," the bed sinks slightly beside me, and I know he has sat down there, "I'm going to tell him about my affair with Sadira. She blackmailed me saying she would tell my brother everything, but in this case, I'll be the one to speak first. I know I was wrong to keep my father's wife as my mistress, but..."

I open my eyes, waiting for him to continue speaking.

"But what?" I murmur, apprehensive.

"But what I have with her needs to end. What we had is in the past, since our marriage..." Again, he lets the sentence trail off.

He lifts his hand and brushes the tips of his fingers against my cheek.

"Since our marriage?" I encourage him to continue.

"Don't get me wrong, but you were quite strange always around your aunt Zenda, head down, whispering when no one could hear you speak. I thought you would be a dead weight in bed, that I wouldn't feel anything seeing you naked. And today, with your parents here, I realized why you were like that. I lost count of how many times Esmail reprimanded you with just his eyes, and I'm almost certain he scolded you during the farewell hugs and greetings."

I don't respond, just bite my lip in confirmation. He continues speaking:

"I was wrong about you, and I won't lie, I planned to have you as my wife and her as my mistress, but well..." He lets a forced smile slip through his lips "everything got out of control when I saw you naked, when I knew that no other man had touched you and that everything about you belongs only to me, every little part, every inch."

"You only wanted me to have a child?" I murmur, feeling like an object.

"Yes," he is direct.

"And I was planning a fairy tale wedding," I whisper to myself.

I close my eyes and swallow my wounded pride.

"Would you prefer I lied?" Abdul asks, and I open my eyes.

"No, the truth helps us grow stronger," my eyes lock onto his intense black ones.

Abdul scratches his beard and puts his hand on the back of his neck, as if thinking about what he should say.

"I want our marriage to be real," I say as I sit on the bed "I don't know how to behave around a man, I don't know how to react in many moments when you're in front of me, I'm not experienced..." I let my sentence trail off. I hold the robe to keep my body covered.

"Experience can be acquired," Abdul murmurs as he moves my hair behind my ear.

"I wasn't raised like your sisters. The only man present in my life was my father. I never felt what it was like to touch someone of the opposite sex. My parents were always extremely strict with our culture, and I just followed it to the letter, avoiding possible punishments," I lower my head, holding one hand with the other, nervously fiddling with my fingers.

"What were the punishments?" Abdul asks, holding my chin and lifting my face.

"It depended. For each rule broken, there was a different warning," I bite my lip, watching him follow my act with his eyes.

"Tell me, Ayda," he asks again.

"Days locked in the punishment room, a square with only a bed and nothing else, making us reflect on our actions. Daddy always said there could be no distractions there for us to reflect. Only one meal a day, confiscating our cell phones. Not being allowed to go outside," I shake my head, recalling the worst that neither I nor my sisters endured "and if he ever found out we had exchanged any contact with a man, he would whip us five times with the whip he makes a point of keeping in the living room for us to see."

"But that's not part of our culture," Abdul's eyes widen.

"As Esmail used to say, that's an adaptation that prepares us to be the ideal wife..." I roll my eyes, wanting to turn my face, but my husband holds it there.

"At this moment, I'd be willing to punch your father for doing this to you. And what about your sisters?" He seemed concerned about the twins.

"Aunt Zenda promised she would find them husbands..."

"Do they want that? Do they want marriage?" I nod, knowing that what they want most is to see themselves far from that place.

"It's strange, because that's my family. My parents were and are strict, but they are my parents. They always did everything for us, and I'm grateful, in a strange way, but I am..."

"Your family now is this one, in this palace. Since we got married, you are my priority," Abdul pulls me onto his lap.

"And should I be grateful for that?" I murmur, sitting sideways on his strong legs.

"Depends..." Abdul holds my head, bringing his face close to mine, our noses brushing against each other.

My husband closes his eyes, letting out a long sigh as we feel his phone continue to vibrate on the bed where I had left it. I turn my face and see his brother's name displayed there.

"It's Hassan," I hand him the phone.

Abdul takes it and answers the call. Even though the phone is at his ear, I can clearly hear Hassan asking Abdul to come to his office immediately.

"Damn it!" My husband puts me back on the bed "I need to go to Hassan. I might be crazy, but I'm almost sure Sadira has spilled the beans."

"Do you want me to come with you?" I hold onto the robe, standing up.

"Stay here, this has nothing to do with you..."

He leaves the room, leaving me alone, but something told me it was best to go with him, so I headed towards the closet.

CHAPTER FIFTEEN

Abdul

I let out a long sigh as I enter my brother's office. All I want at this moment is to be in my room, in the arms of my sweet wife, but here I am.

My eyes sweep the room and settle on Sadira. Damn it! The fact that she is here says it all. Hassan already knows.

I close the door behind me, put my hand in my pants pocket, and walk towards Hassan's desk.

"Sit down, my brother," Hassan gestures to the empty chair in front of the desk, next to Sadira.

"I'm fine here..." I murmur, a bit hesitantly, but I remain behind the back of the empty chair.

"I assume you know what this is about," Hassan begins. "Honestly, my brother, I expected this from anyone but you..."

"I'm sorry to disappoint you," I declare firmly, acknowledging my mistake. "My intention was to tell you the truth."

"That's not what Sadira told me," I raise an eyebrow at what Hassan said.

"And may I know what she said?" I turn my face toward the woman.

"Every story has two sides. What do you have to say, Abdul?" Hassan does not respond to what the woman told him.

"I believe we both made mistakes in this relationship, and now that I'm married, I'm not willing to have a mistress..."

67

"Funny, because Sadira said she tried to break off several times, and you blackmailed her," I widen my eyes.

The woman had the audacity to take a handkerchief and wipe her eyes as if she were crying.

"Wait, what?" I ask, not understanding.

"There's no point in hiding it. Your brother already knows everything. You took advantage of the time of weakness when your father passed away. I asked several times to face the world together and make our love visible to everyone, but apparently, I was the only one who loved. Remember when I found out about your marriage and asked to end things? That's when the threats started. I can't take it anymore, Abdul. Either acknowledge me or leave me," she sniffles, wiping her nose. For Allah, what a crazy story that was!

"Allah, Allah," I run my hand through my hair, somewhat irritated. "Did you believe this, Hassan?"

My brother scratches his beard, rubbing his chin, without answering my question, just analyzing the situation.

I look back at Sadira.

"Why are you making up these things? We never talked about committing to each other; we always knew the scandal this could cause. And as far as I remember, it was always consensual. I don't absolve myself of guilt, but I don't give you the right to make up lies..."

"Why did you come back to the palace, Sadira?" Hassan interrupts, asking the woman.

"He," she looks at me, "said it would be more impossible to go to the mansion, so he demanded that I come to him."

"Oh!" She is distorting everything and, on top of that, crying.

Her crying even seems quite real.

"Brother?" Hassan calls my attention.

"That's not true. Yesterday, I revealed to her that I no longer wanted this. Since I got married, I have had nothing more with her; I have been faithful to my wife. I did consider the possibility of keeping a mistress,

THE SHEIKH'S HIDDEN HEART

and I admit my mistakes. But I wanted to end everything, and it seems that nothing is going as I planned," I shake my head in disbelief at all this drama.

Sadira even sniffs in front of her innocent-theatrical act in this whole story.

"What do you say about this, Sadira?" my brother puts his hands together on the mahogany desk.

"Why are you lying when all I ever wanted was to be loved by you?"

"Huh?" I widen my eyes again. Where is she getting this story from?

"What do you suggest for this situation?" Hassan asks.

I notice that my brother isn't giving his opinion, which is rather strange even for him, who is always intrusive and extremely controlling.

"I suggest that Sadira go back to her home..." I'm interrupted by her speaking.

"I refuse to go back; I want you to take me as your second wife," a laugh echoes in the back of my throat.

"Are you out of your mind? That's impossible; you were married to my father..."

"Technically, nothing prevents it, although it is possible that people will talk, after all, you had a child with my father and were his stepmother."

Damn, at this moment when Hassan should be possessive about his family and against this madness, he is on the fence, playing undecided.

"See? We can continue together," Sadira wipes her eyes with the handkerchief. The woman looks devastated as if she were fighting for the great love of her life.

She always said that our relationship could not be discovered by anyone and that she didn't want to get involved in another marriage to avoid being trapped again. She always made it clear her opinion about living independently without a man by her side to answer to. Why now? Why exactly now that I'm married?

"Abdul?" Hassan calls me again.

"Seriously, Hassan, are you in favor of this crazy story?"

"I don't know what your intentions are. They tried to separate my wife from me; I don't want to make the same mistake with you. That's why I'm asking what your choice is. If you love Sadira, I will go along with it, even though I think it's a tremendous madness. Just talking about this subject is already madness, but I love my wife and would hate for anyone to separate me from her..."

I let out a long sigh, I have the answer on the tip of my tongue and would have responded if someone hadn't knocked on the door. Hassan asked to come in, and through the door, I see my wife, which makes my eyebrow arch.

What is Ayda doing here? If I remember correctly, I told her to stay in the room.

"Great, now we have what was missing," Sadira whispers.

"It's better if you leave, Ayda," my brother sounds a bit serious with her.

"Ayda knows everything, Hassan. We were talking about this very subject before I came here," I extend my hand for her to come to my side.

"Then if she knows, I believe we can proceed with the matter and get this over with," my brother murmurs somewhat impatiently.

"Sadira," I call the woman sitting in the chair, intertwining my fingers with my wife's, feeling her cold hand. "There was never any affectionate feeling between us, and you always emphasized that. I don't understand. What's the reason for all this?"

Ayda's hand tightens on mine; I didn't want to expose her to this.

"Is it just having the girl for one night and you're already in love with her?" Sadira rolls her eyes.

"I didn't want to expose you to this, Sadira. We didn't need to air this relationship to my brother; we could have resolved it between us. I didn't think this could happen, but I want my wife and will do everything in my power to make her happy. I'm sorry..."

I'm interrupted when she stands up abruptly.

"I wonder what our family will think when this gets exposed to everyone..."

"Our family won't think anything," Hassan stands up from his chair. "We won't take this matter further. Your children and my siblings will be just as disappointed with their mother as with their brother. Is that what you want, Sadira?"

"No," she murmurs in response to Hassan's authoritative tone.

"Now answer me, don't lie. If I find out that you lied, there will be consequences. Who is telling the truth?" Everyone knows that one does not lie to an emir. He always finds out the truth.

"I lied, Emir, I lied because I was jealous, and I didn't want to admit that my life is changing. I don't love Abdul; I just wanted him to brighten up my routine," the woman lowers her head.

I turn my face, Ayda's eyes are fixed on the situation.

"That's just what I needed..." Hassan whispers so quietly that I don't know if everyone present hears.

"I think we have nothing more to discuss on this subject," My eyes meet my brother's.

"Sadira?" Hassan calls her attention.

"Yes, Emir, everything's fine. I won't trouble our family anymore."

"You will always be welcome at the Zabeel palace," Hassan declares to her.

The woman nods and makes a slight bow without looking in my direction.

"Ayda, go to our room. I need to speak briefly alone with my brother," I ask my wife as I see my brother sitting back down.

I know I owe him an apology and an explanation about all this madness.

Ayda nods and exits the room.

CHAPTER SIXTEEN

Ayda

I leave the office with my head down, reflecting on the recent events: Abdul chose me. He could have had Sadira as his second wife, but he chose me. Abdul wants only me as his wife.

Right there, in front of his brother and his ex-mistress, he made it clear that he wants me.

"There you are," I'm startled when I turn my body and see Sadira leaning against the wall in the hallway near our room.

"What do you want?" I murmur.

"You insolent girl," she pushes off the wall and walks towards me.

"Accept it, Sadira," I lift my head, looking up at her. "He doesn't want you anymore."

"That's because you're nothing but a foolish girl. Men tend to like younger women until they get tired of them," she says, widening my eyes with her words.

"He won't get tired of me, and if you'll excuse me, I need to go," I dodge her. I want to go to my room.

I don't pay attention until I feel her hand gripping my wrist.

"We're not finished talking..."

"We have nothing to talk about," I look back over my shoulder at her and try to pull my arm away, but she dug her nails into my skin, making me gasp in pain.

"Oh, we do," she declares with a mocking tone.

"Do what the emir instructed, go back to your home and leave me alone," I try to pull my hand away, but it's in vain.

"My home is where my family is, and they are here. That means I can stay here."

I draw in a deep breath, feeling her fingers still digging into my wrist, and realizing she wouldn't let go, I raised my other hand without thinking. With all the strength I had at that moment, I slapped her face with a loud crack.

"Are you crazy?" She finally lets go of my hand and holds her face where I had slapped her.

At that moment, I notice the presence of Maya and Malika, who join us.

"What's going on, Ayda?" Mali is the first to ask me.

"Don't you see what this crazy woman did?" Sadira wipes her face.

"Why did you hit her, Ayda?" My mother-in-law directs the question to me.

"It was a defensive move, just that," I rub my other hand on my wrist where she had gripped and it still hurts.

"Defense from what, against me?" Sadira plays innocent.

My eyes meet Malika's, and fortunately, she seems to be understanding everything that's happening.

"Where are Hassan and Abdul?" Mali asks.

"In the emir's office," I murmur.

"Did he tell you that you requested a private meeting? Did you have it?" Malika, the emir's wife, asks Sadira.

"Yes, I already had it."

Malika looks back at me as if she wants to know if I was also present at the meeting. Being a true lady, she takes her place as the emir's wife, the woman with the most influential voice in this palace.

I nod to her, making it clear that I was present and that I knew part of what was agreed upon between them.

"I ask that you do what my husband required, Sadira. I bet that being here talking to Ayda was not one of the requirements."

"How can you stand by her, princess?" The woman, discontent, looks at Malika.

"I stand by the truth and know everything that happens in this palace," Mali looks at the woman with a certain air of superiority. "I even know about you and Abdul, so I ask you to protect our family's name and accept that there is nothing between you anymore. Men always end up choosing to be with one woman when the passion instinct hits them."

"How?" Maya almost stutters, not understanding.

"Oh, it's nothing dear..." Sadira looks at Abdul's mother, trying to deflect.

"No," my mother-in-law cuts her off. "I want to know, I've always seen you looking at my son with other eyes. Was it only after our husband died that you became Abdul's lover, Sadira!?"

Maya shakes her head in disbelief.

"Your son seems like a boy who doesn't take responsibility. I mean, he really doesn't, just running away..."

"I think we've come to a conclusion: he doesn't want you, you only wanted him to satisfy your desires, and you got jealous when Ayda entered his life. Now what? Do you want to be his second wife?" Malika connects the dots and addresses the topic they had discussed in Hassan's office.

"You're quite smart, girl," Sadira responds with a mocking smile.

"Abdul doesn't want you anymore, and you've made it clear you don't love him. Why don't we just end this once and for all?" I ask, my voice a bit louder than I'm used to speaking.

"Sadira, he is my son..." Maya sighs with regret.

"An adult son fully capable of marital acts," Sadira never lowers her moral stance.

"We were friends above all else, I trusted you," Maya's voice is somewhat sad.

"We'll still be friends," Sadira shrugs. "And you know what? Abdul isn't worth all this trouble. You can keep him. I don't really want him..."

She lets the sentence die when we notice the two men approaching.

"What's going on here?" Hassan asks with an imposing voice.

"Your mother was catching up on the events," Sadira responds, tilting her chin to see Abdul's reaction upon discovering that his mother already knew everything.

My eyes meet my husband's, and I can see the moment he lets out a long sigh. He walks behind the women, coming towards me, and stops by my side.

"I think this matter is settled for today. I believe we've sorted everything out. I want this to be resolved in this palace. Sadira, I expect you to respect me just as I have always respected you. But from now on, I don't want anyone mentioning this again. You must respect my wife; she has nothing to do with this. Among all of us, she is the only innocent one. She was thrust into this as my wife, and if I've chosen to be faithful to her, it's because I respect her and I demand the same respect from everyone here!"

With my husband's hand on my back, I feel the relief of all the accumulated tension.

"I hope everyone understood perfectly every word I've spoken," my husband reiterates.

"Yes, we understand, and out of respect for Abdul's princess, this matter is forbidden here. And, Sadira, our palace will always have its doors open to you. I will always take care of you and all my brothers," Hassan speaks authoritatively.

"Thank you, emir," Sadira murmurs. "I'm leaving now; there's nothing for me here. My destiny is to wander around, maybe exploring other cultures..."

The woman lets the sentence trail off, gives one of her peculiar smiles, and leaves the place without saying goodbye.

I can finally exhale, relieved, thanking Allah that this situation has passed.

"It's late; I believe we all need to retire," Maya says, her gaze fixed on Abdul. "Tomorrow, I want to have a private talk with you, young man."

Abdul rolls his eyes and nods as we all head to our respective rooms.

CHAPTER SIXTEEN

Ayda

"I'm sorry for this," Abdul says with a sigh as he enters our room.

"I just want this matter to be over," I murmur, running my hand through my hair and removing the *hijab* from my loose hair underneath.

"Why did you go after me in the office?" I turn my body to see Abdul walking slowly towards me.

"I was afraid of what might happen," I bite the tip of my lip.

"You shouldn't have gone there," Abdul holds my chin, tilting it towards his face.

"I didn't want to accept that she would say something untrue..."

"Sadira has always been very selfish; that's her nature. She didn't accept it when I ended things with her. With her ego wounded, she wanted to prove to me that she was the ideal woman," his thumb caresses my chin.

"And who is the ideal woman for you?" I bite the tip of my lip, my curiosity sharpening all my senses.

"Still asking?"

He lets a small smile show on his lips.

His face descends slightly, and he kisses my lips with a gentle, slow, and delicate touch.

"I think hearing it from your mouth makes it all more real," I blink slowly.

"Do you want me to say what you already know?" he raises an eyebrow, pulling his face slightly away from mine. "That you are mine, that I desire you with all my strength, that I was a complete fool when I said I only wanted to put a baby in your womb? My resistance to always claim I didn't want a woman by my side made me believe that you would be nothing more than a stumbling block. How foolish I am... Who controls matters of the heart?"

I raise my hand and touch his cheek, feeling his soft beard against my fingers.

"I was wrong about you, my princess," he continues.

"I think I gave good reasons for everyone to doubt me," I make a face.

"And now I see that they just repressed the wonderful woman you are. Please, never hold back from me, never hide anything from me, and, most importantly, when your parents came to this palace, you don't have to bow your head to any reprimands from them. You are a woman now, my woman, and as your husband, I give you the freedom to always hold your head high and voice your opinions. We all want to hear your voice, Ayda," I close my eyes, storing each of his words in my memory.

"I always knew you were my ideal Sheikh," I murmur, opening my eyes and finding his eyes fixed on me.

"Did you?" Abdul drops his casual tone.

"Yes, your brother Hassan carries a heavy burden while you carry the lightness of the palace, and it was you I found myself thinking about most of the time. I would look for you in the rooms and hated when Aunt Zenda would make me dance to attract the emir's attention when I wanted to be dancing to catch yours. You were never there paying attention because you were playing with one of your younger brothers."

He lets a half-smile appear on his face.

"Turn around, my princess," I do as he says and feel his fingers on my back, unzipping my tunic. "Well, I must confess, to me, you were the mirror of Zenda, and, well, Zenda is somewhat annoying."

I turn my face to look over my shoulder.

"If it weren't for your brother, we'd never be here," I murmur, reflective.

"Probably," my tunic falls to my feet, Abdul holds my shoulder, making me turn towards him. "And I would miss out on all this vision, all these curves that only I have worshipped with my eyes."

I try to cover myself, but he holds my hand. His eyes travel down my body, examining every part. My nipple hardens under his covetous gaze.

"Never cover yourself in front of me. I love your body, I love every part of your skin, and in just one night that we've been together, I am certain that I will be the only man to see you like this. Only I will be able to touch you, you are mine, Ayda, all mine. You were promised to me by mistake, and now I will never let you go," Abdul holds my waist, his warm hand trailing down my skin, sending shivers across every part of me.

He lets go of my hand, opens the first buttons of his shirt, and asks me to do the rest. With trembling fingers, I undo each button and pull the shirt out of his pants, sliding it down his arm, feeling his muscles.

There he was, bare-chested in front of me, a broad chest with a few seemingly trimmed hairs.

The epitome of perfect masculinity.

"Do you like what you see?" he murmurs, noticing my curiosity.

"You're handsome," I whisper.

"Not more than you. Now, take off my pants," I swallow, looking down and seeing his member outlined against his pants.

Abdul holds my finger, guiding it to the button of his pants, helps me open it, then I unzip it.

I pull the fabric down his somewhat thick legs, my fingers trembling all the while.

I don't pull down his underwear, and he remains with it on, just as I stay with my panties.

"And now?" I lift my eyes, seeking his guidance.

"Now pull down my underwear," I widen my eyes at his request.

"*But..., but...*" I stammer, nothing coming out due to my embarrassment.

"Do it... Nothing makes me want your hands on me more," I bite my lip, hearing his voice. "Kneel, Ayda..." he requests with a husky voice.

I do as instructed, supporting my body on my knee and, with my cold fingers holding the waistband, I pull down the underwear over his leg and free his penis, which springs out, making me salivate and widen my eyes even more.

I continue with what I was doing. I removed the underwear and Abdul takes another step, stopping right in front of me, his member almost touching my face.

"Put it in your mouth."

"*Ho-how*?" I stammer.

"Suck my cock, Ayda," he says again.

He grabs my hair and makes a ponytail with his hands, guiding my face towards his member.

"Abdul," I murmur his name, terrified.

"My sweet princess, there's nothing I want more than your mouth on my cock, just suck it, don't use your teeth, hold it in your hand, feel it, see how painfully hard I am for you."

I lower my eyes to his member and hold it in my hand, feeling every part, every bit of it.

"Move your hand up and down," I do as he says.

Going up and down until he pushes my head, making it clear that he wants me to take him into my mouth.

With my hands holding it, I take it into my mouth, my lips circling around it, and I go as far as I can. I taste a slight salty flavor in my mouth.

"Use your tongue," Abdul murmurs with a hoarse voice.

And that's what I do. I circle my tongue around it, sucking eagerly, Abdul guiding my head deeper, I raise my eyes, finding his face fixed on mine, his intense black eyes analyzing me.

I gag when he presses for me to go deeper, my eyes tearing up, seeing a smile spreading on his lips.

"So tasty," he groans, gripping my hair.

I continue sucking, circling my tongue.

Going back and forth in various movements, he never lets go of my head, always assisting.

"I'm not going to come in your mouth, and if you don't stop now, I won't be able to hold back," pulling my hair up, he makes me stand.

He releases my hair, holds my waist, lowers his face, and joins our lips in a slow kiss. Tongues intertwine, his lips nibble mine.

"My taste is wonderful in your mouth," he lifts me into his arms, laying me on the bed and coming on top of me.

His hand moves down my waist, pulls down my panties, and tears them with ease.

"Damn, how I dreamed of burying myself in your curves again," he groans, joining our lips in a slow kiss.

Abdul presses his body against mine, I open my legs and feel his penis brush against my entrance.

"This time it won't be as painful," he murmurs between kisses, his hand goes to our center, and his fingers trace my vaginal lips. "*Ah*, so wet and tasty..."

I didn't have time to say anything before his member was inside me, entering my walls, sliding, moving in slow motions.

"I could live inside this pussy, so hot and tight, AH!" Abdul groans.

I bite my lip, feeling him claim me as his own, loving his hands on my body and the way he worships me.

As our lips connect, the slow kiss becomes urgent, the slow thrusts become more constant and rough, his pelvis crashing into my body.

Surrendering to that mix of emotions, I gave in. I roll my eyes as if I'm touching the sky, writhing, moaning his name somewhat loudly.

"AYDA!" he calls out my name and I soon feel his warm release taking over.

We surrender to each other, and he collapses on top of me. We lie there for long seconds, feeling each other's breathing calm.

"Come bathe with me," he whispers, pulling out of me.

He extends his hand and, before I expect it, lifts me into his arms.

I lay my head on his warm chest and close my eyes amid the exhaustion of that crazy day.

CHAPTER EIGHTEEN

Ayda

ONE MONTH LATER...

That same sensation takes over me, the knot in my stomach, the nausea.

I open my eyes and stare at the white ceiling of my room.

Placing my hand over my mouth, I run to the bathroom, where I immediately crouch down and get on my knees. I can feel my husband's hand in my hair, moving it aside.

"Abdul, no..." I don't have time to finish as I start vomiting everything up.

Here I was again, throwing up everything I hadn't eaten, enduring yet another of my morning sickness bouts.

It was just nausea, that's what I always told myself.

"Remember, in sickness and in health," my husband murmurs.

I take the cloth he handed me and wipe my mouth. There was nothing to throw up as I had just woken up and my stomach was empty.

"When will this end?" I murmur, with his help getting up.

"The doctor said the first few months are like this, soon it will all pass," Abdul says, tucking a strand of hair behind my ear.

I nod to what I already knew. I turn my body towards the sink to rinse my mouth. Through the mirror, I see my husband constantly analyzing me as if he were monitoring me.

"You know my nausea is only in the mornings, right?" I declare, looking through the mirror.

"Just in case, I prefer to stay here and monitor everything," he winks.

"This baby hasn't even been born yet and is already causing trouble," I shake my head, smiling.

"This boy is showing what he's made of."

I wipe my mouth and braid my hair to the side.

"You know it could be a girl, right?" I ask, walking towards him while tying the end of my braid.

"It could be, but inside there is a boy," he touches my belly, and I bite my lip feeling his touch.

I lift my face, and his hand immediately caresses my cheek. It's been a few days since I discovered my pregnancy, and since then, I've been having terrible morning sickness. The doctor prescribed some medications, but nothing seems to work, so I'm just accepting it and praying it will pass with time.

My mother-in-law is ecstatic to know there are two grandchildren on the way here in this palace, one from Malika and Hassan, and now, another from my husband and me.

"Shall we have our coffee?" Abdul asks, holding my hand and leading us to the closet, where we change clothes in a pleasant atmosphere. Finally, I put on my *hijab*, covering my hair.

"Do you think I'll be able to feel it move soon?" Abdul asks impatiently.

"You know it will take a few more weeks," I make a face at his excitement.

Abdul rolls his eyes, walking towards me, and holds my face, giving me a long kiss.

"I never thought I'd be married, let alone be a father," he murmurs with his lips against mine.

"I have to admit, you're quite the husband, I think you spent too many years refusing to be one," I smile amidst the kiss.

"I didn't delay, I was just waiting for the perfect moment to have the perfect wife in my arms."

I lift my hand to caress his beard and close my eyes, inhaling his masculine scent, that unique scent he has, the same scent that drives me wild every time I smell it.

"I love you so much, my Sheikh..." I whisper.

"I never tire of hearing you say that, please repeat it."

Since we declared our love for each other, it's been as if everything has become lighter, more real, there are no secrets between us; it's been just the two of us from the beginning.

"*I love you, love you, love you, love you...*" my voice is muffled by his kiss.

The kiss starts slow, with his tongue invading my mouth, exploring every corner and sucking my lip, then he declares:

"I am the happiest man to have you by my side. Nothing I do will be enough to make up for my past with you, but in our present and future, I will do everything in my power to make you the happiest woman in the world, just as you make me, simply by existing, simply by giving me the best gift a man could receive," he touches my belly again.

Sometimes I believe Abdul is more excited about this pregnancy than I am. He is always touching my belly, always talking to our baby.

Abdul is a wonderful husband. When he mentions that he didn't want to be a father and husband, it seems ironic because he is more present than any other man I've ever known.

Even when I'm sick, he is there, every time I have my nausea, he is there holding my hair. Always repeating to me: in health and in sickness.

"You really don't exist, my Sheikh," I smile amidst our kiss.

Arab men can be controlling, possessive, and oppressive, but they are the most loving when they are in love with their wives.

He holds my hand as we leave the room.

"The palace feels so strange in this silence," I murmur, missing our family members.

"Soon they'll be back, and you'll miss the silence," Abdul teases, his fingers intertwined with mine.

He doesn't care about decorum, always showing his affection, holding my hand, giving winks. Except for kisses, we never do this in front of our family members.

We arrive in the breakfast room; it's empty, with only two seats, mine and my husband's.

The whole palace went to Elahe's wedding with her new husband, Khalil.

I really wanted to go, but Abdul decided it was better to stay at our palace, and my nausea wasn't cooperating for us to go out.

My cousin, now also my sister-in-law, was very anxious about this moment, and I understand her, given her past, knowing that her new husband doesn't know anything about what happened to her. This could go badly; Khalil might reject her. May *Allah* protect Elahe.

"Have you heard any news about how the wedding is going?" I ask as he pulls out my chair.

"All I know is from Hassan; he can't wait to get back to Zabeel. We know Hassan hates being away from his emirate," Abdul says, sitting down across from me.

"Today is the last day of the wedding, soon they will be back," I murmur thoughtfully.

"At the latest tomorrow," Abdul rolls his eyes as I smile.

CHAPTER NINETEEN

Abdul

A FEW DAYS LATER...

"Has Elahe sent any news?" I ask Hassan about our sister, who fled from her husband.

"Yes, she arrived safely in California. I just hope she doesn't do anything crazy over there," Hassan closes his laptop.

I let out a long sigh, getting up from the chair in front of his desk, seeing him do the same.

"Khalil left the palace earlier this morning," I murmur, recalling the disturbed man searching for the wife who had run away from him.

"I would be the same in his place, but above all, Elahe is our sister, and I will do everything for her, but that's not what worries me the most," Hassan walks past his desk.

"Did they consummate the marriage?" I ask.

"According to what she said, yes..."

"So she might have fled carrying his child in her womb," I shake my head.

"That could make the situation even more complicated. She may have run away from her problems now, but they always come back," Hassan scratches his beard, heading towards the door, and I follow him out of the office.

Our family is in newspapers all over the world. Elahe's disappearance is headlines in various media outlets. The only luck is that my sister was never seen without her *hijab*, so she surely took it off.

Everyone at the Zabeel palace knows where Elahe is, but they are all loyal to her and haven't mentioned her to her husband or his family.

"I just hope this doesn't interfere with my good relations with Fazza; I depend on him for many transfers," Hassan concludes as he goes down the stairs.

We descend the stairs; the atmosphere throughout the palace was very tense with Khalil's presence and his distress over not knowing where his wife was. Our secret must not be revealed to him.

Now that he is gone, it seems like everything has become lighter; after all, he left without discovering anything about Elahe.

This was her wish, and it seems he rejected her without even caring about her opinion. And we all know that Hassan does everything for her. She was our first sister, and from the time she was a baby, she was the darling of the palace and remains so, even as a grown woman.

We enter the room, where I spot my wife, who is always the first person I notice when I enter a room.

My princess, the woman who carries my child in her womb, is having horrible mornings and going through all this with tranquility.

Ayda is my calm, my safe haven, where I know I can go and she will be there with one of her beautiful smiles.

Everything happened suddenly. I, who always swore I would never love anyone, who always made it clear that being a father wasn't in my plans, am now here, completely in love with her, carrying an entire world on my shoulders just to see her smile.

There was no way not to love her, no way not to desire her. At first, she might have seemed like a helpless little mouse, but once she was away from those who repressed her, she became a woman as stunning as a beautiful flower in bloom.

I walked over to her and sat down beside her. My hand soon reached for hers, intertwining my fingers with hers.

Mom soon entered the room, this woman always has a smile on her face since she found out she will be a grandmother of two children.

Of course, I got a good lecture from her about Sadira, and Mom made me promise, on my knees, that I would never betray my wife, as if that were a possibility for me; I desire no other woman but her. My princess.

"Did you hear the latest?" Malika announces loudly so everyone in the room can hear, then continues speaking once she has their attention "Sadira is on a cruise, I don't know where, and there's more..."

Everyone went silent, I turned my face, noticing a smile on my wife's lips, making it clear that she already knew. Malika and Ayda are inseparable, always sharing everything as if they were two sisters.

This was all thanks to a little push from Elahe, I know, my sister, who is also Ayda's cousin, asked Malika to give Ayda a chance and not to hold a grudge against her for everything her mother Zenda did to the family.

"Zenda is with her; it seems they are both on a cruise," Malika concludes.

"Now they are exactly where they like to be," My mother teases.

"Aunt Zenda loves to be the center of attention," Ayda says with a smile.

"I pity the passengers on that cruise," Hassan scratches his beard amidst the laughter.

Soon everyone was laughing at the situation, finding it somewhat hilarious.

Sadira never interfered in my marriage again; she even came to visit us and, although she didn't speak to me or my wife, she respects us.

Zenda, Ayda's crazy aunt and my father's second wife, hasn't caused any more trouble; on the contrary, she was happy about the news of our baby on the way. According to her, she was the one who united us, even though we all know she wanted Ayda to become Hassan's second wife. It was under my brother's influence that I married Ayda, as he practically forced me into this marriage. Perhaps this is the most pleasurable obligation I have ever had.

I don't know what our tomorrow will bring, I don't know the outcome of my sister's disappearance.

We may be the center of attention right now, but that doesn't matter to me, because I have her by my side, I have my wife.

I may have bitten my tongue when I made it clear that I would never love her, that I would never desire her, because I desire her with all my strength and I love her with everything that dwells within me.

Is there any way not to love Ayda?

The most beautiful creature I have ever held in my arms, the woman I adore to worship every day, every hour.

My princess, my wife, the mother of my future child.

EPILOGUE

Ayda

I place my hand on my belly and let out a long sigh. The final weeks of pregnancy are wearing me out. My feet are swollen, and my mood is swinging in surreal ways.

I descended the last flight of stairs, hearing the soft cry of Latifa, Hassan and Malika's newborn baby girl.

Entering the room, I see the emir with the little girl, that tangle of black hair, in his lap.

Latifa looks almost like a doll, so small and delicate, with all her features from her mother. Since her birth, Hassan hasn't left his wife and daughter's side, and this event made the newspapers forget about my cousin's disappearance.

Elahe is still in California living the life of an American. When Abdul revealed that she wasn't even wearing the *hijab*, it scared me, but it's what Elahe wants. However, there's a catch to all of this—she's pregnant, Elahe is carrying a baby in her womb, the child of the husband she fled from.

"Malika, I really envy you for already having your daughter in your arms," I murmur, out of breath.

I soon lift my face and see my husband by my side.

"Didn't I tell you to rest? You keep going up and down these stairs," my husband warns me, making everyone in the room look at us.

"I'm not staying in that room alone, and besides, the midwife said the more I walk, the better it is for our baby," I say. As the days pass, I stopped referring to the baby as possibly a girl.

Abdul was so convinced it was a boy that I gave in, but I made it clear that if it's a girl, he'll be the one to blame for already naming the child.

"Our son Hakan will be a good boy and spare his mother from all suffering..."

"May *Allah* hear that." I smile at him, seeing him wink.

Abdul guides me to the sofa where I sit next to Malika.

"Gentlemen," I raise my face upon seeing one of the palace officials appear at the door, "Mr. Esmail and his wife Raja are here."

"Let them in," Hassan responds without lifting his eyes from the daughter.

I wonder what my parents want. Maybe it's just another visit, one of the many they've made frequently lately.

"Beloved daughter," my mother is the first to enter, coming toward me.

I didn't stand up to greet them as the weight of my belly prevents me.

I received a greeting from my dad and mom, who soon sat down in front of us on one of the many sofas scattered around the large room.

"What a lovely little creature you have, emir," my mom says with a smile, looking at the man holding the daughter, keeping her snug in his white robe.

"Latifa will be the most beautiful child of the seven emirates," my father murmurs, proud of his daughter.

"I have no doubt about that," my mother replies.

I wait for them to say something, but nothing was mentioned.

"Dad, Mom, is there something that brought you here today?" I ask.

The fact that I have a voice in this palace has always made my father look at me with a frown, but he has never shown any refusal, knowing that if I am like this, it's because my husband allowed it.

Abdul hates when I am silent; he always emphasizes that I deserve to be heard, that my voice is too beautiful to be whispered, and for that reason, I have complete freedom to speak as I please.

"Well, ah..." my father tries to start speaking, but nothing comes out.

"In-laws?" Abdul prompts him to continue.

"I have arranged suitors for your sisters, and they want them. They come from noble families, do not hold the title of Sheikh, but they are well-off. There is only one catch to all of this," my father begins to rub one hand against the other.

"And what would the problem be, the dowry? I'll pay it if that's what's holding things up," Abdul declares promptly.

"Oh, my son-in-law is so generous," my father joins his hands in an act of glory. "I thought we'd lose this opportunity, and Soraia and Selma want them. They are two brothers just like them and will be able to live together in the same mansion as their family."

"If that is their wish, know that I will cover all the expenses for this union," my husband crosses his legs.

Hassan didn't hold him back, and like the emir, my husband carries great wealth, only he doesn't flaunt it as much as his brother.

"By Allah," my father stands up, going to my husband's front to kneel, but is stopped by Abdul, who holds his hand.

"We are family; I am not your emir to kneel before. I will always do everything in my power to see my wife's family well," Abdul declares seriously.

My father makes a brief bow, even though it wasn't necessary.

"My twins will finally be able to get married," my mother murmurs.

I watch the two of them, who initially did everything to make me adhere to all my husband's rules in silence, now realizing that things don't quite work that way in this palace.

It's as if the men hold the power, but beside them stands the woman, the one who guides them in wisdom, and it's on them that they place all their trust.

The foundation of the Zabeel palace is the woman beside her Sheikh.

Abdul takes my hand again, as he always does, his fingers continuously intertwined with mine, making it clear that I am his princess.

"You look radiant, my daughter," my mother changes the subject.

"I feel like a huge ball," I declare amid my gasping sighs, as if our baby is consuming even the air I breathe.

Latifa started fussing in her father's arms, who promptly handed the baby over to her mother. They pass the girl from one lap to the other. Only when the baby needs feeding or a diaper change does the father get a break, as no one has yet managed to detach him from his daughter.

Malika has a natural way with the baby, as if she was born to be a mother.

ONE MONTH LATER...

THE CRYING FILLED THE entire room.

Abdul, sitting by my side, holds my hand, making it clear that he is there with me.

My eyes, already unable to contain so many tears, cry even more seeing the baby with his dirty black hair and blood-stained skin. My little one...

"It's a boy," the midwife wraps him in a blanket and hands him to my husband.

"I always knew it was a boy," Abdul holds him in his arms—"my Hakan, the light of my life."

My sheikh holds him to his chest without worrying about getting dirty. Hakan's cries calm down as his father whispers the *Adhan* in his right ear, introducing the baby to our Allah, welcoming him to this world.

My eyes are blurred with tears. I know my world was there: my husband and my little son.

It was a long fifteen hours of labor, but in the end, it was worth it. It was worth having him here.

Abdul, with tears in his eyes, completed the moment by handing the little one to me.

And there, I saw him for the first time clearly.

"My little son..." I murmur, my voice choked with emotion.

"How I love you both," Abdul runs his finger along my cheek "you gave me the best gift I could receive, our son, the fruit of our love."

I smile, looking at that tiny bundle in my lap.

My baby, mine and Abdul's.

And in the end, all our effort was worth it.

I am madly in love with my protective Sheikh.

THE END!

Did you love *The Sheikh's Hidden Heart*? Then you should read *Surrender to the Sheikh* by Amara Holt!

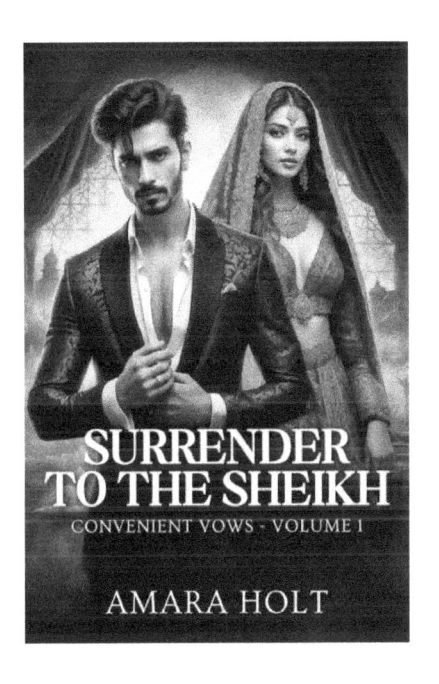

Surrender to the Sheikh

When **Kaled**, a powerful CEO and notorious playboy, is forced to step into his brother's shoes as **Sheikh** of Rheadur, his life of freedom and indulgence is suddenly threatened. As the second in line to the throne, Kaled never wanted the crown—or the crushing responsibility of ruling an entire nation. But tradition demands that he marry, and Kaled refuses to be tied down in a loveless union. Instead, he concocts a bold plan: a **marriage of convenience**, where passion is allowed but love is off-limits.

Adeela has spent her life under the iron grip of a patriarchal society, yearning for a taste of **freedom**. With dreams of reuniting with her American mother, Adeela is desperate for a way out. When the future

Sheikh offers her an **irresistible deal**—one that could give her the independence she craves—she seizes the opportunity.

But as the sparks between them ignite, Adeela finds it harder and harder to protect her heart from Kaled's raw and **magnetic charm**. He never wanted to be Sheikh, but now he must rule his people and **surrender** to the woman who captivates him in ways he never expected.

In *Surrender to the Sheikh*, duty collides with **desire**, and a union born of necessity becomes a love story for the ages. Will Kaled and Adeela be able to resist the powerful pull between them, or will they surrender to the passion that threatens to consume them both?

About the Author

Amara Holt is a storyteller whose novels immerse readers in a whirlwind of suspense, action, romance and adventure. With a keen eye for detail and a talent for crafting intricate plots, Amara captivates her audience with every twist and turn. Her compelling characters and atmospheric settings transport readers to thrilling worlds where danger lurks around every corner.